FAE FRACTURED

BOOK TWO IN THE FAE BLOODLINES SERIES

ROSE GARCIA

For Liz Ferry!

I'm so glad my late is your early!

Published by Rose Garcia Books

Cover Design by Get Cover Designs

Editing by Liz Ferry

Map Illustration by Cartographybird

TO THE FAR NORTH
THE EVENING SEA
STRONG HAVEN WEST
THE
QUIETUS VALLEY
HIGH
MAJESTIC CHASM
CUESTA
FAR TO THE SOUTH

THE FAE REALM OF

FAEVENLY

TORCH LAKE

STRONG HAVEN EAST

MOTHER RIVERS

SUMMIT RANGE

GREEN FALLS

SAND LUFF

THE GREAT COVE

THE MORNING SEA

1 MALENA

The sky had darkened, but it wasn't the night that stole my breath—it was the body lying at my feet. The sprinkling of fireflies that hovered over the Strong Haven palace grounds, and the moonlight and stars overhead, illuminated the area well enough for me to see the lifeless form of my favorite maid servant on the ground.

Maid Rell's eyes were wide, her mouth open, and an arrow pierced her head. She was devoid of life, looking as if she could have been a statue tumbled over. A statue with blood smeared down its face. I turned away from the sight, hating that I had ordered her death. But I hated even more that she had made me do it.

She had supported Celyse, the one I thought was my twin sister, and Celyse and Rook and their band of traitors had attempted to overtake my mother and my father. But they were not successful. Rook lay dead in the Great Hall, and Celyse and her rebel survivors had been banished to the Sublands. My father had also been sent, but for different reasons. He had consorted with a human, produced an illegitimate heir, and held her out as my twin.

My gut twisted tight. The treachery I had been raised on was unraveling.

How could he have done that? And how could my mother have gone along with such a horrific ruse? Humans were our mortal enemy, inferior in every way. If I could, I would ask her why she had tolerated Father's wrongdoings, but she had fallen into a state of undeath when Rook took her name from her.

Now, I was alone, my family name thrown under a dark cloud. I was going to do whatever I could to shine a light on it again. No matter who I had to destroy to do it. And my first step would be claiming my birthright.

"My Lady Malena, what do you want to do with the body of Maid Rell?" asked one of the guards.

With my head held high, I turned to face the guard. I moved slowly and deliberately, keeping my expression smooth and inscrutable, each step filled with foreboding and purpose. If I was to solidify myself in my new role, I would have to start now. It is what Mother would have done.

"You will address me as High Queen," I commanded. "Understood?"

The guard bowed low, as did the others around him. "Yes, High Queen," he responded, his words laced with fear and apology. "I meant no disrespect."

One of the wolfbeasts licked my hand, then pressed his large body against my leg, as if approving of my decision to put the guard in his place. I slipped my fingers through its thick fur and stroked its head, plotting my next move.

I had ordered the execution of Maid Rell. I had obliterated the shimmer Celyse's vile human had stepped through during his and Celyse's attempt to escape to the human realm. But I needed something bigger. An overt act to declare my position. Everyone needed to know that I was the High Queen now and ruler of Faevenly. Even with my mother in her current state, and my father turned out, the Strong name would hold.

I would not let a band of rebels take what was mine.

But first, I needed to replace Jaid, the former head of security for the Strong palace—a guard to stand over the others. Unlike Jaid, this guard would be loyal above all else. The one before me, with his long dark braided hair and deep emerald eyes, looked younger than Jaid. Perhaps that would make him eager to please. Young guards were always willing to do whatever necessary to move up the ranks.

"What is your name, guard?" I asked.

He tipped his head. "Windon, High Queen."

I kept my gaze on him but could tell the other guards were waiting to see what I would say next. The tension hung thick between them and me. Which I liked. They needed to fear me. I wondered if Windon was the one whose arrow had lodged through Maid Rell's head. Something about his stance and attentiveness suggested so.

"Windon, is that your arrow?" I asked, motioning to the body at my feet.

"It is, High Queen."

With a raised brow, I nodded at him with satisfaction. "I commend you on your loyalty to the crown."

He bowed again. "Thank you, High Queen."

I swished the train of my gold-laced dress behind me and faced Strong Haven Palace. Today Celyse was to have wed, and the Strong family had been set to celebrate with all the provinces. Instead, bodies were strewn across the floor of the ceremonial hall. Blood and innards were scattered throughout. Anger swirled inside me at the thought of my beloved home being violated so. Those responsible would pay, and severely.

But how?

If my mother were here, she would know just the thing. But she was not here. I had no advisor, no one from whom I could seek counsel. Not that seeking counsel would be easy. Fae were cunning deceivers, and traitors could still be in my midst. I could only rely on myself. And the quicker I got my house in order, the better.

I brought my attention back to Windon. "Put together a team of guards and gather Maid Rell's body and the others that have fallen. Ride them into the heart of Strong Haven, to the village center, and burn them. Let the onlookers know that I am now High Queen, and swift punishment will befall those who stand against me and this house."

The guard nodded. "Yes, High Queen. And the

prisoners that are being sent to the Sublands? What of them?"

I had banished them until I could think of a suitable punishment for the traitorous group. I did not think them worthy of a quick death. Especially when it came to my father and Celyse. They would need a sentence befitting their wrongs.

I raised my chin. "They will remain imprisoned while I contemplate proper punishment."

Another bow. "Yes, High Queen."

Windon took no time ordering the other guards into action, and soon they had lifted Maid Rell and were carrying her toward the palace. I stayed behind, letting the guards handle the gathering of the dead. I did not want to see my precious Strong Haven in such a state.

My wolfbeast stayed close, and another joined us. I kept a hand on each of them, grateful for the comfort and protection they provided as my thoughts drifted to the melee I had barely survived, shocked at the sheer numbers of those who had turned against House Strong. A proper investigation would have to be launched. A band of rebels was never as small as it seemed. There had to be others involved.

"Malena," a voice called.

Alexander approached. If not for his house, House Kane, I did not know what would have happened to me. I was beyond grateful but did not wish to overly show it. He too needed to know his place.

Straightening my posture, I faced him with authority. "Alexander, how does it fare inside?"

He placed his hand on my shoulder. "It fares well. The bodies are being gathered and placed in a carriage, and a team of maid servants are busy cleaning."

"And my mother?" I asked.

"The High Queen has been placed in her chambers," he said. "We await further instructions."

The High Queen? Did he not know anything? I flicked his hand off me. "I am the High Queen now, Alexander. You would do well to remember that. Especially if you still desire to court me."

He did not miss a beat. "Of course, my love. I simply did not know if you were ready to don the title so quickly. That is all." He brushed a strand of silver hair from my face. "As for courting you, I desire much more than that."

The thing about Alexander was that sometimes he was *too* much like me—consumed with ambition for title and recognition. Not that it was bad to have those things. But I also desired love and affection. Did he? Gazing into his brilliant blue eyes that sparkled in contrast to his jet-black hair, I hoped the answer to my question was yes.

"Well," he prodded, moving in a little closer. "I realize this may not be the best time to say so, but will you allow me to take steps beyond courtship?"

Alexander had been my in my heart since I was a little girl. From the first time I met him when he and his family came to the palace for a visit, and every time I saw him after, an affection for him worked its way through me, like a glorious slow-moving sunrise. And this courting season was supposed to have been my time to shine.

But everything had been ruined.

Alexander stroked my cheek. "Will you let me stand beside you, Malena? Let me care for you and shoulder burdens with you?" He cupped my face with his strong hands. "Will you let me be there for you in your time of need? Will you please choose me?"

Did he really want me? Or did he only want to be High King? And did it even matter? I placed my hands on top of his. Courting season had long gone, and another season had been thrust upon me. A season of rule and establishment. I would need him and his house to succeed. And he knew it.

"You know I choose you, Alexander. It has always been you."

His lips parted and he leaned forward for a kiss but was interrupted when a guard approached. "High Queen, my apologies." The guard cleared his throat. "Windon believes it best for you to inspect the bodies before departure."

Alexander backed away, putting on an air of duty. "I will see to it, High Queen."

I nodded, grateful for him to take on the task. "Thank you, Alexander. I will be there shortly."

After they left, I closed my eyes and drew in several deep, long breaths, letting the woodsy air fill my lungs as the cool night breeze worked its way through my long silver strands. And as the wind departed, I thought I heard it whisper my name.

"Malena."

My eyes snapped open. Was an attacker out here? Did a rebel from the wedding slip out undetected? My gaze darted about, but there was no one around. Even my wolfbeasts had gone off somewhere. Strange that they had done that, and I had not noticed.

"Malena," the whisper said again. "Come to me."

My body froze as fear prickled the back of my neck.

"Come, Malena."

A tug pulled me away from the palace, forcing me to walk into the woods, my body operating on a command that was not my own. And I was powerless to disobey.

"Keep coming."

With each step, my mind scrambled for ideas on how to escape my course, but I could not slow my stride nor deviate from my path. With the moonlight illuminating my footsteps, I neared the edge of the manicured grounds and crossed into the wild shadowy woods. I was almost upon a cluster of thick trees when I spotted a figure shrouded in darkness.

Tall. Lean. Dressed in all black with the lightest skin and sparkling white eyes. I came to a halt before Draven the witch.

I let out a sharp breath and uttered, "Draven."

The witch approached, his black cloak drifting behind him. "Malena."

My words failed me for a few seconds as I thought of the human named Julio and how he had used Draven's name against him and expelled him from the palace. "I thought you were—"

"Cast out? Of the palace and its grounds, yes. But here, beyond the landscaped borders, no. The fool human had no idea how to wield his gifts. Luckily for me, and luckily for you, I am still around. And when his magic wanes, as it most assuredly will, I will once again have access to Strong Haven. But for now, I am here in the shadow."

Mother had always trusted Draven, and that meant I could too. At least, I thought I could. Gazing into his sinister yet beautiful face, I pushed my doubts aside because I needed him. With a witch to do my bidding and support my cause, no one could possibly stand against me.

"I am glad to see you, Draven," I said.

He studied my face. "And I am glad to see you."

I thought of commanding him to address me as High Queen, but thought the better of it. I doubted anyone commanded him to do anything. I clasped my hands in front of me, not knowing what to say, but I did not have to worry about that. Draven knew what to say.

"Listen carefully, Malena. I cannot step foot on palace grounds yet, but I can meet you anywhere else. All you have to do is call me."

I twisted my hands together in front of me. "So when you say I should call you, how?"

"However you want. With a word, a thought, or even a wish. I will always hear you."

"It is that easy?" I asked, my mind processing what it meant to have a telepathic bond with Draven.

He moved in closer, his sparkling eyes fixed on me with menacing intensity. I nearly backed away on instinct but caught myself and held my ground. I was the High Queen, and needed to act the part. Besides, he was too beautiful not to behold.

"Yes, it is that easy . . . *if* you assume your mother's role."

He shifted away from me. This time, I advanced toward him on my own, not needing him to spell me into motion. "Do you mean taking on the title of High Queen? If so, I have already done that, as it is my birthright. Unless you mean something else."

Draven circled me; his steps so soft he made no sound at all. Or maybe he was floating. "Have you ever wondered about my relationship with your mother?"

I blinked. I had most certainly wondered but had never asked. Mother kept many things private. But maybe Draven would divulge an answer. I swallowed. "I have wondered."

With his gaze glued on me, he explained, "When your mother was your age, she came to me and asked me to help her win your father's heart. At the time, he was heir apparent of Strong Haven, and she was but a mere lady of the smallest house of Sand Bluff. Trite and meaningless. She desired so much more than her station and set her sights on your father, wanting nothing more than to rule by his side as High Queen. And she was willing to do anything to get what she wanted."

I sucked in my breath, knowing full well what he was saying. "She bargained with you?"

"She did."

Bargains were treacherous. But a bargain with the likes of Draven? That was infinitely worse. Grasping to understand how my mother could have done such a thing, it occurred to me that with my mother's state, perhaps the bargain was null.

Calling forth my bravery, I challenged him. "She is undead, surely any bargain she struck with you is no longer."

He kept his crystal stare on me. "As long as she breathes air, the bargain holds."

"Oh," I muttered. My curiosity about the bargain mounted with each second. With my new status, I thought I should know. "Well, I am High Queen now. You will tell me what it is."

He smiled; his beautiful face laced with pure evil. "I will do what I will. And you will do what I say."

Our eyes locked. Every inch of me said to defy him, but it also said that I needed him. Did I want his support that badly? I had feared Draven for as long as I could remember. I had considered him like a childhood monster lurking under a bed or in a dark corner-the darkest evil in all the land. Even though my mother had gone to him, it did not mean I had to. I was the

High Queen. I had Alexander and the full support of his house.

"I will not enter into a bargain with you," I said, my voice sounding small even though I had tried to make it big.

His lips tugged into a wicked smile. "I am not asking, Malena. But if you want my assistance, the way I assisted your mother, you must step into her role, and that means assuming her agreements. But *you* must be the one to ask. It is not for me to do."

"I see," I whispered.

His face was so close to mine, I could smell his cool breath. It reminded me of a winter morning, the kind that preceded an ice storm.

"Do you have an ask for me, Malena?"

A clatter rang out behind me. Boots pounded against the dirt as voices frantically called out my name. My hands clutched the fabric of my golden dress as I looked back in the direction of Strong Haven Palace, then whipped my head back to Draven. "What is happening? Do you know?"

He stayed close. "Are you asking for my assistance?"

My heart started racing. Heat worked its way up my neck and into my face. I had been groomed to step into the role of High Queen, and now my time had come. I needed to not be afraid. I needed to be more like my mother.

Right?

The shouting increased in urgency. Somewhere in

the distance, the wolfbeasts started howling. Something horrible had happened.

"Malena, thank the stars, you are safe!" Alexander called.

Looking over my shoulder, I saw him and a troop of guards rushing over to me. I turned back to face Draven, but he had vanished. Alexander stepped into his place.

"Safe? What do you mean?" I asked.

"It is Rook. He is missing."

I gasped. "Missing? I thought he was dead!"

The guards swooped in, bows and arrows drawn, daggers and swords brandished.

"He was," Alexander answered. "I checked his body myself. But somewhere between loading the dead and cleaning the palace, he disappeared."

Fear cascaded inside of me. Rook was the one who had led the attack against me and my family. He was the one who had taken my mother's name away. He deserved a thousand deaths, but now he was free. And I was probably his next target. If anyone could protect me from Rook's threat, it was Draven.

While Alexander and the guards scrambled about, devising their plan to locate Rook, I gazed in the direction I was sure Draven had disappeared to, a dark shadowy spot deep in the trees.

"Alexander, wait here," I said, stepping away from him.

He held my arm. "Malena, I mean, High Queen. It is not safe."

I placed my hand on top of his. "I will be fine. I am only going a few paces. Trust me."

He dropped his hand and watched as I walked into the woods. As I neared the shadows, I mustered my courage and whispered in my lowest voice. "Draven. If you can hear me... I ask for your assistance."

I detected movement within the darkness, like a shadow within a shadow, as if the trees were moving.

"Do you step into your mother's role, Malena?" Draven asked, his voice whispering all around me. "Do you assume her bargain?"

This was it, my chance to step into greatness, and I needed to take it. Especially now with Rook missing. Pushing my fears aside, I said, "Yes, I step into my mother's role, and all that comes with it."

Cool air caressed my face. This time, Draven's voice that floated all around me sounded as if it were at my ear. As if he stood beside me, even though there was nothing there. At least, nothing my eye could detect.

"How may I be of assistance, High Queen?"

In the distance, I heard the guards tramping through the woods, looking for Rook. I knew deep down they would not find him. Rook was too cunning and devious. Draven, on the other hand, could.

"I want you to find Rook Cailean and kill him."

A few seconds of silence followed before he breathed, "As you wish, High Queen."

2
JULIO

My spine tingled as I approached the shimmery portal from the fae realm to the human realm. It wasn't the sizzle from the supernatural gateway, or my body preparing for the weightlessness I was sure to feel when I passed through. It was something else. Something bad. A feeling of dread, as if something horrible was about to happen. I tried to stop myself so I could warn Celyse who was standing behind me, but couldn't. I was already in motion.

My body sucked into the portal, and I landed face first on asphalt. Pain from the concrete vibrated through my teeth, across my head, and down my body. I let out a groan, then rolled over to catch Celyse's fall, but the shimmery glow disappeared.

And there was no Celyse.

I scrambled to my feet and spun around, searching for any glimpse of her or Faevenly, but found none. Instead, I was on the sidewalk of an ordinary suburban neighborhood. Two-story red brick homes lined the streets. Cars were parked in the driveways. The sky was dark, but streetlights illuminated the area.

"Young man?"

An older woman in sweatpants and a sweatshirt with a small, fluffy white dog walking across the street came into view. She stopped short of crossing over to me.

"Young man, are you okay?"

I brought my hand to my mouth to make sure my teeth were intact, and they were. "Yes, ma'am. I'm okay. I just, uh, fell down."

She kept her distance. "From where? I didn't even see you there a second ago."

"Oh." A nervous laugh came out of me. "I was, uh, down here"—I pointed at the nearby bushes— "tying my shoe."

She considered my explanation for a few seconds before she said, "I see." She continued walking. "Well, you be careful with that."

"Yes, ma'am."

I walked in the opposite direction from the lady, panic rising inside of me with each step. I had no idea where I was or what had happened to Celyse. Not to mention the fact that my best friend, Manny, had been imprisoned in the fae realm, along with Leto, Parlan, Ferna, and Jaid. I drew my cell phone out of my back pocket, but it was dead. Shoving it back in place, I rounded the corner, then continued weaving my way up and down the sidewalks. Eventually, I emerged out of the neighborhood and onto a street. Neon lights from a convenience store sprang into view.

Picking up my pace, I hurried over, but stopped short of entering. I needed to get myself together. I steadied my breathing, thinking of my plan, then started pacing around. I'd ask to borrow someone's phone, then call my mom. I knew she'd be freaked because I'd been gone for days now after my house had been attacked. She had probably called the cops too. The sooner I could talk to her, the better.

With my nerves somewhat settled, I was about to walk into the store when a hazy figure walked my way —it was a guy around my age with a bullet hole in his head. Most ghosts that found their way to me hadn't been murdered like that. I turned away from him, but he kept walking and floated right through me. I clutched my chest, gasping at the tingly rush of cold.

"Hey, dude," he said, having no idea what he had done. "I can't find my car. I think I'm lost. Can you help me?"

I gulped. He was one of the dead that didn't know he was dead. My mom had told me about ghosts like that, but I had never encountered one. "I'm sorry, but I can't. I'm not from around here."

"Oh, okay. Thanks, though," he said, walking away from me, continuing to look for his car.

The door to the convenience store swung open followed by the jingle of a bell, and I practically jumped out of my skin. A slender guy came out, with a broom in his hand. His eyes widened when he saw me.

"What in the hell happened to you?" He glanced about the parking lot. "You okay?"

I stopped myself from touching my face, remembering the gash on my forehead from the car crash and the cuts from Leto's bow-and-arrow training session. I was probably bruised from when my face smashed against the concrete too.

I rubbed the back of my neck. "I'm fine. Just a rough couple of days."

"Really rough," the guy added.

He seemed nice enough, and I thought he might even want to help me. I pulled my phone out of my pocket and flashed it at him. "My phone is dead, and I'm far from home. I really need to make a call. Mind if I use yours?"

"Not at all." He opened the door and waved for me to follow him. He went behind the counter, leaned his broom against the wall, and passed his phone over. He also handed me a cold bottle of water.

"Thanks," I said with a smile, grateful to have something to drink. My throat was bone dry.

After taking a chug of the ice-cold liquid, I set the bottle down and called my mom. After a few rings, a guy answered.

"Uh, hello?" I said, wondering if I had the wrong number.

"Julio!" It was Trent, my cousin from Houston. I wasn't expecting him to answer, so hadn't recognized his voice.

"Hey, *primo*," I said in a low voice.

"Jesus, Julio! Where are you? Are you okay?"

"I'm fine, I'm fine. I'm uh . . ." I looked at the guy at the counter, who was not so inconspicuously listening to my conversation. "What city is this?"

He cocked an eyebrow. "Baltimore."

"Baltimore?" Trent asked. "You're in Baltimore?"

"Apparently," I exhaled, turning away from the counter. "It's a really long story. Where's my mom?"

"In the bedroom. She's been worried sick. She hasn't eaten or slept since you've been gone, and she finally just dozed off. My mom is in there with her. Want me to wake her?"

I swallowed, thinking for sure my mom would want to talk to me. "Yeah, go wake her."

"Okay." The phone shuffled around, and I could tell Trent was walking.

"Are y'all at my house?" I asked. "Is it," I swallowed, "still standing?"

"It's still standing, but barely. And no, we're not there. We're at *Tio* Tony's and *Tia* Maria's house. The family has all gathered. We've been praying rosaries since you've been gone . . . and eating lots of menudo."

His half-hearted attempt at humor by adding the menudo comment fell far short of making me feel better. In fact, it made me feel worse because I felt awful that the entire family was together worrying about me. I was an only child, and so was Trent. But my mom had four siblings and they all had tons of kids. Whenever there was a special occasion or even a crisis, the family always got together at *Tio* Tony's and *Tia* Maria's house because it was the biggest. And most gatherings involved pots of menudo and mounds of tortillas.

"I'm going into the room now," Trent whispered. I

kept quiet and heard him moving around. He said in a low voice, "It's Julio."

"Julio?" I heard his mom say.

More rustling, and more whispering. And then I heard the unmistakable voice of my mom. "*¿Es mi hijo?*" A lump formed in my throat and hot tears stung my eyes. I could hear her grabbing the phone as she cried through thick sobs, "*¡Mijo!*"

"Mom," I choked out. "I'm okay. I'm in Baltimore."

She cried into the phone for what seemed like a solid minute until finally she called out, "He's okay! *¡Gracias a Dios!* He's in Baltimore!" The room erupted in chatter. She yelled at someone to give her a pen and then said, "Tell me where you are, and we'll get on the next flight."

I turned around and faced the guy behind the counter. "Um, can you tell me the address here?"

"You want your mom to come get you . . . from here?"

"Yeah." I nodded with a half shrug. "I can wait outside."

The guy stared at me for a few long seconds before he rattled off the address. I relayed it to my mom while she jotted it down.

"Trenius," she whispered to Trent, using his full name like all the *tios* and *tias* did. "Get two plane tickets. Hurry." Then she asked me, in a halfway calmed voice, "*Mijo*, are you safe?"

I walked away from the counter and stood by the chips. "Yeah, I'm safe."

"Good." She fell silent for a few seconds, the kind of silence that hung thick with worry and fear. I knew in my gut what she was going to say next.

"*Mijo* . . . is Manny with you?"

A fresh wave of tears rushed my eyes. I swallowed hard as I fought to keep them in. "He's . . . not with me. He, he . . ." I couldn't get any more words out.

She soothed me with a shush. "It's okay, *mijo.* It's okay. We'll talk about it when I get there. But he *is* okay, right?"

I envisioned Manny with Leto, Jaid, Parlan and Ferna, being banished away to the Sublands. I had to believe he was okay, that Leto would keep him safe. My hand went to my shirt, and I patted my cross that hung underneath. "I think so."

"Good, *mijo.*" More ruffling sounded around her, and more chattering broke out in the background. "Here, I've got the flight info. Trenius and I will be leaving Austin at six in the morning, arriving in Baltimore at ten in the morning. It's the earliest flight. We'll head straight to you after we land."

I rubbed the tears from my eyes. "Thanks, Mom. I'll see you then."

"Yes, God willing."

She hung up and I stared at the phone for a bit, struggling to keep my emotions in check. When I thought I had a handle on myself, I went back to the counter and passed the phone back to the guy.

"Thanks," I mumbled, keeping my eyes cast down

as I headed for the door, thinking I could sleep in a nearby alley or something.

"Hey, wait up," the guy called out.

Stopping in my tracks, I backed up a bit. The guy had dark hair and an unshaven face. He only looked a few years older than me but carried a whole lot of sorrow and heartache in his green eyes. After spending many years helping my mom with her *curandera* business, I could tell a lot about a person from their eyes.

"Tonight's your lucky night. This place is open twenty-four hours, and I'm working the graveyard shift. There's a cot in the back storage room, and you can bunk there if you want. There's also a bathroom." He held out another bottle of water. "Water is on me, and so are the snacks. Help yourself."

Relief washed over me, because even though I was willing to sleep outside, I didn't exactly want to. Especially with a dead guy roaming around. I moved closer to get the water and read his name tag. "Fleet," I said, thinking it an interesting name. "I'm Julio. Thank you for your offer. I really appreciate it."

"You bet."

With the fresh bottle of water in one hand, I surveyed the snack aisle and grabbed two bags of pretzels with the other, then headed for the storage room, eager to be alone with my thoughts.

"Hey," Fleet said before I ducked in. "One more thing."

"Yeah?"

"Whatever is going on with you, you'd better find

your fight. No matter what." He crossed his arms. "I've seen a lot of crap, and I've had some run-ins with some messed up people, and I promise you one thing—good always wins in the end. But only if you fight like hell. You got me?"

The weight of everything that had happened crushed me hard, but hearing this guy's words filled me with hope. He was right. I needed to find my fight. I'd figure out a way to get back to Faevenly. I'd save Celyse, Manny, and the others.

I had to.

I nodded at Fleet. "I got you."

3
CELYSE

The wheels creaked and the carriage rocked as it carried me away from Strong Haven Palace. Clad in my torn and damp gold wedding dress, I thought of everything that had happened in the Great Hall—Draven showing up, Jaid revealing himself to be on the side of my allies, Julio fighting beside me.

A shiver of disbelief shook me, my mind hardly able to believe it. Not to mention my wound and my first kiss. I opened my hand and gazed at the white quill sitting in my palm. Draven's red magic had hovered over everyone, immobilizing us. Yet somehow, Julio's blue light overtook it.

"How did you do that?" I muttered.

Julio had used the same blue energy to protect me when a cloaked figure attacked us after our car crash. If Julio had been able to perform such magic, I had to trust he was safe in the human realm and could use his gifts to find his way back to Faevenly.

Until then, I needed to focus on me. And my first order of business was figuring out how to escape.

I shifted to the side of the carriage and peeked through the opening, scanning the road ahead and behind. The wheels clattered softly against the packed dirt, the steady rhythm blending with the rustle of wind through the trees. No other carriages followed, which was good.

Turning toward the front, I squinted into the dark. The moon and stars cast just enough light to glint off a driver's arm, the leather of his sleeve catching the faint glow. I leaned to the opposite window and caught sight of another arm.

"Two drivers," I muttered, sitting back in my seat. "I can handle two." At least, I hoped I could handle two. I was an expert with the sword and the bow and arrow, but I had not yet mastered hand-to-hand combat. I patted my thigh, wishing I still had my dagger that now lay somewhere in the Great Hall, but ready to act without it.

Scooting back to the opening, I leaned my head out. "Driver, I need you to stop, please." The carriage carried on without any sign of slowing. "Driver! Stop!"

The driver muttered. A few seconds later, the horses slowed to a halt. The carriage dipped down then rocked back up as the two drivers jumped off. Their footsteps crunched over to me, and my door jerked open. Before me stood a driver in black pants, a white top, and a black jacket. Behind him stood a guard in the customary attire of green pants and a black shirt. He looked vaguely familiar, as if I had seen him with Jaid's troops in the Great Hall. But it appeared he did not share Jaid's alliance, as he held a bow and pointed an arrow at me.

Thunderation. I was not expecting to face an arrow, though I should have known better. A new plan quickly formed in my head. Forget fighting. I needed to run, but not now. I needed to get into the woods.

"What is it, prisoner?" the driver asked.

Prisoner? It sounded so strange to be addressed as prisoner when hours earlier I was princess, daughter of the High King and High Queen. My new title turned my stomach.

"I am no prisoner," I hissed, narrowing my eyes at the pair.

The guard held his aim. "You are whatever the new High Queen says you are. You would do well to cooperate."

High Queen? It seemed Malena had wasted no time stepping into her new role. Typical.

Focusing on my new strategy, I peered at the dark woods. I had spent so much time with trees, I knew I could weave in and out of any wooded area quickly. But first, I needed the guard to escort me over there.

"I require a moment of privacy in the woods to tend to my business," I announced, wondering how they would react to my request.

The driver looked over his shoulder at the guard.

"I will not venture far beyond the tree line, and I will be quick," I offered, making their decision easy.

The driver and the guard exchanged another glance.

"Or would you prefer I relieve myself in the carriage?" I asked in a threatening tone. "I am most confident Malena—or I guess I should say the new High Queen—would not appreciate having her carriage soiled. The seats are made of the finest black velvet, and it would be quite an endeavor to have them recovered. Do you want her wrath on you for that?"

The driver shrugged slightly to the guard. After a few moments, the guard nodded. "Fine. I will accompany you."

"If you must," I replied, expecting no less from him.

The driver stepped out of my way, giving me room to climb out of the carriage. He stayed back while the guard and I started walking. The cool breeze wrapped around me, sending a strand of silver hair across my face. I swiped it away and kept a steady pace.

"I am defenseless, yet you feel the need to keep that arrow on me?" I asked, scanning the different-sized trees, wondering which spot looked the best for me to carry out my escape plan.

"I am required to do so," he answered.

"And what if I told you that you are on the wrong side?" I paused, letting my words sink in. "That you are taking orders from someone who should not be in power?"

"I would tell you to mind your tongue, unless you desire your life ended here and now," he grunted.

There was no reasoning with him, so I kept quiet as we continued into the woods. After a few long strides, we arrived at a spot far enough inside the tree line to make it difficult for the driver to see. But with the arrow close, I would need to disarm the guard before taking off.

I stopped and turned to face him. "Will you kindly face away from me?"

The guard hesitated, as if considering my request. "I will not turn away, but I will avert my eyes."

"Thank you, I guess," I said with my best fake smile.

He cast his eyes downward, his aim following his gaze. In that split second, I lunged, grabbed his arrow, and twisted it free. The stunned guard frowned, then charged me with his bow. I deflected with the arrow and whacked at him, his bow and my arrow locking against each other.

"You are on the wrong side of this fight," I groaned, pushing all my weight against his.

"You are as good as dead," he threatened.

I thought he had a point; he was seconds away from overpowering me. Using a tactic Jaid taught me when we were young, I let my knees buckle and ducked. The guard fell forward, and I reared upward, sending him tumbling over me. Wasting no time, I sprinted. I weaved in and out of the trees, dodging limbs and branches. I expected to hear boots and hollering, but heard nothing.

Had I knocked the guard out with the tumble? And what about the driver?

I slowed my pace. I listened for any indication I was being pursued when a snapping twig met my ears. Leaves crunched. I pushed my back against a thick tree trunk and held the arrow with a firm grip, ready to attack.

"My Lady? Princess Celyse?" a hushed voice called out.

The voice belonged to Adva, the petite servant from Strong Haven. I'd know it anywhere. She and her brother had been the ones who helped me leave the palace, sending me to the shimmer and to Julio so I could finally uncover the truths that had been hidden from me.

"Adva!" I rushed over to her. "What are you doing out here? There is a guard after me and a driver not far behind!"

I took her arm and pulled, but she resisted. "They are not after you any longer, princess."

Her brother came out from the trees and joined us. "They are sleeping now."

It took a few seconds for his words register. "Sleeping?"

"Yes," he answered, patting a brown leather bag slung from his waist. "I dusted them with sleeping powder."

"It was easy to do to the driver," Adva explained. "Because he was sitting on a rock."

"But harder to do to the guard," the brother continued. "He was running after you and we had to trip him."

"When he fell, we got him," Adva finished with a small smile.

With an exhale, I studied the small-framed, innocent-looking siblings, grateful to see them, but also wondering where they had been. I had been looking for them for days back at the palace. "What happened to you two? How did you end up out here?"

"We will tell you, but we must go to safety before your pursuers wake up." She motioned for me to follow her and began explaining on the way. "The High Queen must have suspected some of the servants were not loyal to her. She started questioning our days and our nights, wanting to know details of every little thing we were doing. Because fae can never lie, we thought it best to leave the palace before it was our turn to be interrogated."

"So we left," Adva's brother concluded, trudging alongside us, "and came out here."

"But how did you know to come find me?" I asked.

"We did not. We are merely staying here in the woods, waiting for our friends to join us. Then we saw the carriage. And you came out, looking like . . ." Adva slowed her pace and motioned to my dress, unable to say the words she must have been thinking.

Gazing down at myself, I saw a downtrodden prisoner, with a torn and tattered blood-stained dress, my long hair spilling out of its arrangement. If I had found me, I would feel sorry too.

"We saw you run and knew you were in danger, and we wanted to help," her brother finished.

Before I could ask another question, the words *danger* and *help* struck me. I halted and thought of my father and my friends being held in the Sublands. I eyed the bag of sleeping powders.

"What is it?" Adva asked.

"I have an idea," I muttered. "And I could use your help."

"Of course," the siblings said together.

"Much has happened at Strong Haven since you left. There was a rebellion and a fight. My father and my allies were captured and taken to the Sublands. I am being sent there too."

"By who?" Adva asked.

"By Malena, the new High Queen. She has taken Strong Haven."

Adva and her brother turned to each other with opened mouths and wide eyes.

"I was escaping my captors," I went on. "But now I want to go back to the carriage so that I can be taken to the Sublands. My father and my friends need me. And I need that," I said, pointing at the bag.

Adva's brother looked down. "My sleeping powders?"

"Yes," I hurried out. "And anything else I can conceal under my dress that will help me."

They exchanged surprised glances, then sprang into action. "Follow us," they said, resuming their course with haste.

We did not have to go far before we came upon a clearing with a modest campsite. Stones were placed around the perimeter, like a border. A small pavilion made of cloth took up the space in the middle. Adva lifted the flap on one side, and I entered, marveling at the space. Everything was neat and orderly; there were bedrolls, wooden stools, and a spot in the middle for a small fire.

Adva hurried to a sleeping corner that must have been hers. She rifled through her things and brought out an onyx dagger and a sheath. It looked exactly like mine, but smaller.

"Here," she said, holding it out for me. "Strap this to your thigh."

Her brother sifted through his things too. He handed me a pouch like the one he had at his waist. "Here is a fresh supply of sleeping powders." He pulled at the string. "You can tie this to the sheath. To use the powder, simply flick it in someone's face. Once a person ingests it, they will fall asleep. The more powder you use, the longer the sleep. Be careful to wipe your hands after you use it. You may even use gloves if desired for extra protection, though not necessary."

I had heard of sleeping powder, but had never seen it or tried it. I was already imagining how I could use it to help my friends.

"If you want your captors to take you to the Sublands, you should hurry back," Adva urged, her brown eyes wide with worry. "We did not use much powder on them, so they should be waking soon."

With a nod, I turned away from them and lifted my skirt, strapping the sheath with the dagger around my thigh, then attaching the pouch. Dropping the golden fabric back in place, I patted my stash, satisfied everything was secure and concealed. Now, I needed to get back before the driver and guard awoke. But what would I say to them? How would I even explain them falling asleep? I was not sure but figured I would come up with something when I got there.

We darted from the campsite and back through the woods, retracing our path. We slowed our pace as the fallen body of the guard came into view. He lay face down, eyes closed, his hand still clutching his bow. And then, his legs twitched.

Adva wrung her hands in front of her. "He is waking."

Before Adva could say another word, an idea came to me. I knelt before her brother so that we were eye to eye. "Sprinkle a bit of the powder on my face. Only enough for me to fall asleep for the shortest while."

His brows furrowed for a second, then raised as he understood my plan. He reached into his pouch and moved in close. His soft brown curls had the slightest tinge of yellow at the edges, and tiny freckles dotted his nose and cheeks. I realized I did not know his name.

"Friend, what is your name?" I asked.

He smiled, and a pink blush spread across his cheeks. "Aedon, my lady."

"Thank you, Aedon." I glanced at Adva and nodded at her. "Thank you both for helping me."

"You are most welcome, Princess Celyse," Aedon said. "We pray to the sun and the moon and the stars that you will fare well."

"We do," Adva added.

"Thank you," I said again. "I pray the same for you both."

He raised his fingers, held them steady, then flicked them in front of my face. A hint of lavender mixed with lemon laced its way through my nose with a tickle. In the furthest regions of my mind the sensation of falling pulled at my brain.

WATER SPLASHED ACROSS MY FACE AND MY EYES FLUNG open. The guard came into view, hovering over me against the backdrop of a dark sky and leafy treetops. I sat up with a groan and rubbed the back of my head. "I was . . . asleep?" I muttered. The powder had most certainly done its job.

"You were, as were I and the driver," the guard responded. He helped me up but kept a firm grip on my arm so I would not run away.

The driver came into view. "I do not see anyone," he said.

The guard scanned the woods. "Nor I." He swung his attention back to me. "What is the last thing you remember seeing as you were running away from me?"

"The last thing I saw was the face of a boy," I answered.

The guard studied me. "Where is the arrow you took from me?"

I hid my silent gulp, remembering setting it down

at Adva's and Aedon's campsite. "I must have dropped it." I quickly followed up with my own question. "What is the last thing you remember seeing?"

"I saw the same as you. We both did. A small boy."

"Let us get out of here," the driver implored, his eyes shifting about nervously. "We do not know if what we saw was indeed a boy or something else entirely."

"Something wicked," the guard tacked on, his stare fixed on the trees.

Eyeing the guard's hand on my arm, I said, "I assure you; I will not venture away. Not with wickedness in the woods."

The guard kept his grip. "I am not going to fall for your trickery twice. Now, come."

We went back to the carriage and the driver took his seat in the front. The guard, instead of joining the driver, climbed in and sat next to me. I crossed my arms and scooted over to the edge, keeping my gaze on the darkness outside, not caring if he sat with me because now I desired to go to the Sublands. It was the only way I could help my father and the others.

We traveled in silence, stopping only a few times. As the hours turned into days, the view morphed from green and lush to dry and barren, yet surprisingly beautiful.

We passed colorful rock formations of russet, pink, and orange that emerged from the ground into thick mounds. Some were even narrow and tall like columns. There were also gorges and canyons of auburn, violet, and yellow. With all the vibrant colors, the sky itself seemed bluer than any blue I had ever seen. Even the air smelled purer and fresher than other provinces. I had no idea a landscape of rock and dirt could be so magnificent, as if the gods themselves had used this space as their own personal playground.

On our third day, as the sun began to set, we began traveling downward. The rocks all around lengthened and stretched out, and the horizon started slipping from view.

“We are going into a canyon?” I asked.

“We are,” the guard answered in his monotone voice.

I had visited every province in Faevenly—the rolling meadows of High Meadow under the stewardship of the Kane family, the lush mountains of Summit Range under the stewardship of the Stromm family, the salty beaches of Sand Bluff under the stewardship of the Baffin family, and the expansive mountainous ridges of Cuesta under the stewardship of the Lind family.

But I had never been to the Sublands.

The Sublands, though not a province, was looked after by the Caileans. I wondered, now that Rook was dead, what had become of them. Surely, Malena would have dealt with them swiftly. During my long and slow journey, she had probably sent an envoy to take out the family. I wondered who she would have put in charge in their place, and what punishment she had exacted on my friends. A sinking feeling in my gut told me it was bad. I prayed to the sun and the moon and the stars that I was wrong and they were safe. I did not think I could take the sorrow of losing my father or Jaid. I also did not want any harm to befall Manny, Leto, Ferna, or Parlan.

Forcing myself to push my worries aside, I gazed out the carriage opening, wondering what geometric rock shape I would see next, when I spotted a structure carved into the canyon wall that looked like a house. It was followed by another, and then another, until soon every inch of rock contained a structure of some sort.

"A village of rock?" I murmured.

Some of the edifices were modest square-shaped homes. Others were tall and impressive with elaborate steps and massive doorways. If Maid Rell's teachings had included a lesson on the structures of the Sublands, I had surely missed it.

The village took my breath away.

After not much longer, the carriage rolled to a stop. The guard hopped out and opened the door for me. I climbed out and saw a sizeable crowd, and beyond, the grandest sight of them all. A palace jutted out of the canyon with ornate spires, an expansive door as wide as it was long, and an elaborate stairway that started out wide, then narrowed at the top where a deep dais sprawled out. It reminded me of the grand cathedrals Maid Rell had taught me about during one of my lessons on the human realm.

Taking it all in, my sharp eyes met something else at the top—the unmistakable figures of my father, Jaid, Leto, Ferna, Parlan, and Manny. Their hands were bound behind their backs and gags filled their mouths. My stomach plunged. I knew they were here, but I was not expecting this.

"What is going on?" I asked the guard.

"You shall see," he grunted, gripping my arm and nudging me forward.

I held my head high and kept my back straight as I walked forward. The crowd parted before me and closed back in after I passed. Murmurings broke out in patches, rotating between soft whispers and elevated chatter—the words traitor, human, and vile drifting above the din.

I ignored the insults, making my way slowly up the stairs, keeping my attention on my father. He wore his silver-and-white suit from the wedding, but it was now dusty and stained, all its sparkle and shine grimed over with dirt. Like me, he kept his royal pose—head up, back straight. I could almost hear him telling me not to worry, that everything would be all right.

But I knew better.

My gaze drifted to the others. Jaid was tugging at his bindings with his brow furrowed and jaw clenched. Leto stood motionless, staring at the crowd with fierce intensity. Manny stayed close to Leto, his hair wild and eyes wide. Ferna and Parlan were like Leto, still and observant.

As I reached the dais, my mind turned to the dagger at my thigh, calculating when I should go for it. My fingertips were itching for the hilt, ready to risk everything and go for the weapon, when the massive stone door before me grated open with a groan.

Two figures came out. Alexander Kane and Draven the witch.

My breath hitched. A blast of icy fear shot through me. Where was Lord Cailean? My stare fixed on Draven as the pair walked forward. They stopped before me. Draven stayed one step behind Alexander, legs spread wide, his hood shrouding his face, his black cloak drifting behind him.

I had not even noticed the guard's grip still on my arm until he dropped it, leaving me standing in front of Alexander.

Alexander raised his hand and the crowd hushed. "Kneel, prisoner!" he ordered.

I kept my posture straight, refusing to obey the likes of Alexander Kane. He flicked his hand at the guards, and two rushed me. They clutched my shoulders and shoved me down with brute strength. My knees slammed against the rock as the crowd yelled with approval.

"Prisoner!" he hollered in a booming voice for all to hear. "You have been banished by the High Queen to the Sublands where you will await her judgment!"

Through the roars of approval I spat, "And who are you? What authority do you have here? You are a Kane and your province is High Meadow. You have no authority here."

Alexander's eyes narrowed. "I am soon to be High King, and as such will have authority over all the provinces and lands of Faevenly, including the Sublands," he hissed. "And you are but a lowly prisoner with human blood in your veins. It would behoove you to not challenge me."

I met his stare. "I also have fae blood, Alexander. Royal fae blood."

"There is nothing royal about you." His mouth curled up in a sinister smile. "The bloodline that spawned you ceases today."

What? I whipped my head to my father. A hint of surprise etched across his face, and he glanced at me with sorrow and regret. I thought of all the times he had been there for me, comforted me, and loved me when the High Queen would not.

I turned my attention back to Alexander. "Ceases? What do you mean, ceases?"

He ignored me and motioned to the guard with a flick of fingers. "Move her with the others."

The guard jerked me up by my arm and pulled me back. He shoved me into place next to Manny, then tied my hands behind my back and stuffed my mouth with a leather gag.

Alexander stepped closer to the edge of the dais and addressed the crowd. "Citizens of the Sublands, the new High Queen of Faevenly hereby declares that anyone who stands against her rule will be severely punished! And today, she has asked me to gather you all for a demonstration of her power!"

The crowd cheered so loudly it echoed throughout the canyon, bouncing from end to end. When the cheering died down, Alexander commanded the closest guard. "Bring him forward."

The guard marched over to my father, jabbed him in the back with a staff, and prodded him over to Alexander. The crowd roared even louder. Jaid yanked at his restraints, fighting to break free, but another guard struck him in the gut, sending him to his knees.

"Stop!" I yelled in a garbled tone, lunging forward when a searing jab struck me from behind, sending me to the ground too. Jaid and I exchanged desperate glances.

Alexander stepped back while Draven moved forward. The witch lowered his hood and stared down the crowd with his deadly glower. Everyone quieted, waiting for him to speak.

"I am honored to stand here today on behalf of High Queen Malena Strong and future High King Alexander Kane to exact punishment on this creature for tampering with shimmers and consorting with humans, our mortal enemies, the punishment for both of which is death."

Another roar filled the air. I hardly heard it as I scrambled to rise to my feet but was pushed down again with a boot to my back.

Draven kept his wicked stare on my father and moved in close, leaning toward him. "The High Queen wishes me to convey to you that you have done this. Not her," he said in a low, intimate tone meant only for those on the dais to hear.

Father remained calm and expressionless, refusing

to show the slightest hint of fear, as if telling me and the others he was not afraid, and we should not be either. But fear exploded within me anyway, rocking me deep into my core.

I was about to lose my father.

Draven snapped his cape behind him and drew out a long white spear strapped to his back. He twirled it over his head, aimed for my father's neck, and brought it down with force.

I slammed my eyes shut, unable to watch as my heart shattered into a million pieces.

4
JULIO

Tears streamed down my mom's face when she saw me. I wrapped her small frame into my arms and held her until her sobs slowly subsided. When she was finally under control, she pulled away and looked up at me.

"*Ay, mijo.*" Her fingertips shook as they reached for the cuts and bruises that riddled my face and neck. "*Tu cara.*"

Even my *primo* who was with her, Trent, was overcome with emotion when he saw me, his eyes filling with tears.

"*Es nada,*" I said to her, giving her another hug and pulling in Trent for one too.

After a quick thank you to Fleet for the food and letting me crash at the convenience store, my mom, Trent, and I headed for the airport. Mom suggested we not talk about what had happened until we got to back to Austin, which was fine with me because I was still processing everything, not to mention I was utterly exhausted. I hadn't slept well at all on the cot.

The flight boarded on time, and because we had purchased our tickets last minute, we ended up on the back row. We sidled into our seats, and I angled my body toward the window, resting my head on the wall of the plane.

Worry for Manny and Celyse had settled deep in my gut, but for Celyse, it was much more than a sinking feeling. My heart ached for her, the pain so deep in my chest, it radiated throughout my entire body. I loved her with everything inside of me, and I couldn't lose her. I just couldn't. My mind stayed on her as the plane took off, but sometime midflight, slumber overtook me.

After what seemed like a few minutes, but was really a few hours, a nudge on my arm woke me. "We're here, *mijo*."

I sat upright and rubbed my eyes. "That was fast."

Once we deplaned, I started rehearsing in my mind what I would say to my mom, wondering how she'd react to everything that had happened. As a *curandera*, she'd heard a lot of wild tales, but mine would probably top them all. A fae realm that overlapped the human realm? I doubt she'd heard that one.

Tio Tony lived just outside of Austin in a small town called Elgin. The homes were large one-story ranch style structures, and each one sat on its own acre of land. *Tio* Tony's house was brown brick with green shutters and a circular concrete driveway in the front. Chickens roamed free, and he even had a cow in the backyard. When we got there and walked through the door, I expected the entire family to pounce on me. Instead, no one was there.

"I asked everyone to leave so we could talk alone," my mom explained.

Trent patted my arm. "That's my cue to leave." He kissed my mom on the cheek. "Call when you're ready for us to come back."

"I will, Trenius. Thank you for coming with me," she said.

With a hard swallow, I lowered myself onto the edge of the red leather couch. Mom pulled up a chair and sat across from me. She sighed, and we sat like that for a while before she finally said, "I'm ready for you to tell me everything."

"Everything," I repeated.

"Yes, *mijo*. Everything." Like she did during her *curandera* sessions, she threaded her fingers together and held her hands before her, as if praying. Which, of course, meant she actually *was* silently praying.

I began telling my mom everything. How Celyse appeared through the shimmer, how we got close, how she suddenly stopped visiting me but then months later showed up in the flesh with a wound, and how Manny and I had to take her to Leto's for special medicine.

"Special medicine?" she asked.

"Yeah, special medicine because she was poisoned by a fae arrow."

My mom tilted her head. "*¿Que?*"

"Fae, as in faerie." I shrugged because I didn't exactly know how to explain what fae meant. "It's a magical world that overlays ours. Our world used to interact with their world, but then a war started hundreds of years ago. After the war, the entire human race was mind wiped with something called a glamour so we wouldn't remember them."

She tilted her head. "These fae are not human?"

"No, they're not. But Celyse is actually half human."

She kept her stare on me, absorbing everything I had to say, her eyes bloodshot and puffy from all the pain I had caused her. I dreaded going on because I worried how she'd react to the part about me seeing my dad. But I had to go on.

"Manny and I got her the help she needed. Then, she found out that some of the fae were using portals to take humans as slaves to mine a special rock. She wanted to figure out a way to stop it, but before we could do anything, fae guards came for her and took her back. Manny and I and some good fae that live here in the human realm went to Faevenly to save her and that's when . . ."

My voice drifted as I thought of my dad's ghostly image. Mom placed her hand on my shoulder and held it there. "You can tell me."

"Mom, I was trying to save Celyse and . . . I saw Dad."

She looked frozen, my words chilling her to the bone. "Your father?"

Hot tears stung my eyes, and I swallowed the lump in my throat. "Yes, he's there, in Faevenly, as a ghost. He helped me when an evil witch tried to kill me and the others. I would be dead if not for Dad."

She let go of my shoulder and covered her face, weeping quietly into her hands. "*Mi amor, mi vida.* I knew he didn't leave me. I just knew it."

"I'm so sorry, Mom," I muttered. I leaned over and hugged her tightly, crying with her, feeling awful that I had doubted my father for so many years. I hoped she would forgive me.

When Mom and I separated, she wiped her eyes and gathered herself. I did the same. "And Manny?" she asked. "What happened to Manny?"

A fresh wave of grief and guilt shook me. "He and Celyse," my voice cracked. I took a deep breath and pushed through. "They and the others who were helping me were taken away by Celyse's evil sister Malena. But I got away when I stepped into a portal."

Mom made the sign of the cross, then nodded. "Is that everything?"

Feeling better that I had gotten everything out, I stared at my hands. "Well, there's one more thing. I need to tell you something I discovered about myself."

Mom scooted up close to me. "What is it, *mijo*?"

"You know how we can read auras? And how you always said mine was blue and powerful? Well, you were right. I didn't even know what I was doing, and it shot out of me and protected me and my friends."

She smiled. "You are blessed with gifts from both your father's Avila side of the family, and my Rodriguez side. Your gifts are strong, stronger than anyone in the family, even me, so I am not surprised at all to hear that your gifts came through for you. Not surprised at all."

She hugged me again, and then rose to her feet. She pulled out her phone and started texting.

"Who are you texting?" I asked.

"Trenius. I'm telling him that he and the family can come back. We've got work to do."

"Work?"

"*Sí, mijo*. Work." Her face took on a serious expression. "We are going to get Manny back. We will show the evil fae over there they've messed with the wrong family."

I blew out a sigh of relief and sank into the couch, grateful to have her taking charge. "Yes, we need to get them and quick. There's no telling what that witch will do next. Or Malena."

A few minutes later, the family started returning to the house. They covered me in hugs, fussing over the cuts and bruises on my face and neck. When the last family member arrived, everyone gathered in the kitchen.

I pulled my mom back. "Uh, what's happening? We need to get going on the evil fae, like now."

She patted my cheek. "We will. But we need to eat first. Now come."

Being in the safety of family made me feel better, and the mention of food set my stomach growling. Other than the pretzels at the convenience store in Baltimore, and some airplane cookies, I hadn't eaten since the stew at Leto's house. A meal break seemed like a necessity. Plus, for us, family gatherings always centered around meals.

Everyone crammed into the small lime-green kitchen, taking leftovers out of the fridge and setting up a buffet-style spread of barbecue, potato salad, beans, guacamole, pico de gallo, and tortillas. My mouth watered as the delicious sweet and spicy aroma of the food filled my nose, but then a twinge of despair twisted my gut. I often included Manny in family gatherings. He should've been here with me, filling up his plate and telling jokes. He never passed up a meal and he loved my mom's cooking.

"Julio?"

My attention snapped to *Tia* Maria standing in front of me, handing me a paper plate.

"Oh," I said. "Thank you, *Tia*."

I took the plate. As much as I wanted to pile on the food, I found that I couldn't; my gut was too twisted. But I did take a flour tortilla to nibble on. Trent and I scooted our way around the packed kitchen table and wedged into a spot on the window seat. After a quick prayer, everyone started digging in and catching up. And for a few long minutes, everything felt normal. Like I was a normal guy hanging with my normal family.

But of course, nothing was normal.

When everyone finished eating, my mom got up and grabbed a trash bag and started scooping up the emptied paper plates. Everyone else started putting the food away and wiping down the table and the counters. With everything done, the mood in the room changed as my mom sat down and held her hands together in front of her in a way that signaled everyone needed to listen.

Finally, we were getting somewhere.

"*Mi familia*," she said in a serious tone. "In this family, we have been given gifts from our heavenly Father—we can see things and do things others cannot. And it has always been our calling to use these gifts and help people when they come to us."

Murmurings of assent drifted around the room.

"My Julio is back from another world that overlays our world. It is called Faerie. That is where Manny is right now, along with some good fae folk." Mom met the eyes of every person in the room before continuing. "There are also evil beings in Faerie. These fae mean us harm. It is these evildoers who took my beloved *esposo* from me."

"*¡Dios, no!*" several of my *tias* and *tios* gasped.

Tio Tony shot to his feet. "We must go get him!"

"He is not alive," I interjected. *Tio* Tony lowered himself to his chair with a look of confusion on his face but kept his stare on me. "He's a ghost, *Tio* Tony. And he's the only reason why I'm here." I gulped. "He saved me."

More murmuring broke out. My mom let it go on for a few seconds before she raised her hand to silence the room. She said in low tone, "They have a witch over there."

"An evil and powerful witch," I tacked on.

Mom nodded. "We need to figure out a way to get over there so we can bring Manny home and free the good fae who have been helping Julio."

Mom sat back and a discussion ensued amongst the family about different ways to help. Trent leaned in close to me. "They have a witch?"

I rubbed the back of my neck. "Dude, you don't even know the half of it. The guy is straight up wicked, with a black cloak and a pale face and these crazy eyes that sparkle like freakin' diamonds. I didn't even . . ."

My words cut off as a tingle struck the back of my neck. The kind that signaled danger. My gaze whipped over to my mom and hers to me.

"He's searching for you," my mom whispered.

"I think so," I murmured, feeling it in my bones that Draven was searching for me, somehow using his powers in the human realm.

My gut clenched as Mom shouted orders in Spanish. Everyone started grabbing hands and praying. Trent gaped at me wide-eyed as the house rocked. The sunlight pouring through the windows dimmed. I was waiting for a blast, expecting Draven to kick the door down and fling his red energy at us, but as soon as everything started, it stopped.

Mom looked at me. "It has passed."

The family stopped praying and slowly released hands as the light from outside filtered back into the room. One of my little cousins ran into the room, crying. *Tia* Maria scooped her up and rubbed her back, taking her out of the kitchen.

With the room hushed, I said. "That was the witch. He's the one that attacked me and Manny and my friends at our house."

"He's the one who destroyed your house?" *Tio* Tony asked, fiery anger brewing in his brown eyes.

"Yes."

Tio Tony went off in Spanish, and everyone joined in. But not Mom. She kept her cool, walked to the wall where a picture of the Last Supper hung crooked, and straightened it. She sat back down, her quiet and thoughtful demeanor encouraging others to do the same. Trent and I glanced at each other, then eased back down on the window seat. Not one second later, the doorbell rang.

Trent's eyebrows stitched. "Uhh . . . do you think Draven would ring the bell?"

I wanted to laugh, but then wondered, *would he*?

Before anyone could react, someone in the front room must've opened the door because in strode Manny's dad. He wore his all-blue janitorial uniform—pants, long-sleeved shirt with the hospital emblem on the pocket, thick black belt, and black shoes. Dark circles encased his brown eyes, as if he hadn't slept in days. He was short, like Manny, and had the same sunny disposition. But now, there was no sunshine in him at all. Only heartache and sorrow.

"Julio," he said, with watery eyes. "I am so glad you are home, *mijo*."

"Me too," I whispered. I walked over to him, and an all-too-familiar lump formed in my throat. "I'm so sorry Manny didn't come back with me."

He placed his hands on my shoulders. "I know, *mijo*. I know." He gave me a reassuring squeeze. "It's not your fault. Not at all. I know we'll get him back."

His words lifted the weight bearing down on me. I wrapped him in a a tight hug. "Thank you, Mr. Vela."

I hoped he was right.

5
CELYSE

The guard yanked me up by my arms and held me before Draven. Even though hot tears rolled down my face, I kept a steady gaze on the evil witch.

"Look down, Celyse," he ordered in a threatening tone. "Look at what I have done to your treacherous father."

I kept my stare locked on his, refusing to give him the satisfaction of doing what he wanted, when his arm swooped and his hand grabbed my chin. His long, thin fingers dug into my jaw. The leather in my mouth shifted and gagged me, sending fresh tears to my eyes. He forced my face in the direction of the ground. I kept my gaze raised for as long as I could until his hold tugged my line of sight down so far, my father's bloodied body came into view.

I snapped my eyes shut, the horror of the sight sending my head spinning while my body trembled and my knees weakened. If not for the guard holding me, I would have toppled over.

"This will be you, as you are guilty of the same crime. But not yet," he whispered at my ear. "Not yet."

Draven jerked his hand away from my face. "Take her and the others and put them in their cages."

A guard prodded me forward while another moved Jaid and the others to follow. We were led off the dais and down a narrow set of stairs. When we got to the bottom, a small, dark opening came into view. A few paces in and glowing lights from a row of torches hanging on the walls illuminated our path.

The smell of rock and dirt filled the air, and somewhere there must have been a water source, as the earth beneath my feet gleamed with wetness. We were not far in when the walls widened out, revealing a large circular opening lined with floor to ceiling cages. The guard in front of me came to a halt. He rifled through a pouch at his waist and drew out a thick key. He inserted it into the lock, clicked it open, and swung open the bars. He grabbed my arm and pushed me inside, then locked the door.

Leto, Ferna, Parlan, Manny, and Jaid shuffled by. Jaid gave me a sidelong look and nodded, letting me know he was with me. I stuck my hand through the bars, my fingertips grazing his shirt. They were placed together in a cell across from me.

The guard locked them in, then ordered, "Stick out your hands."

With their hands held out, the guard undid the bindings around their wrists. When he finished, he came over to me to do the same. With my hands free, I yanked the leather gag out of my mouth, taking in slow, deep breaths.

The guard sneered at us, then walked away, disappearing from view.

"Celyse," Jaid said, in a sympathetic voice. "Are you all right?"

Unable to answer, I turned away from him and the others and retreated to the back wall. I sunk to the cave floor and covered my face, letting my tears flow freely, not even believing what had happened to my father.

He had been taken away from me before my eyes, in the most brutal way, and I could not stop it. I also feared what was next.

When my tears finally stopped and I had pulled myself together enough to face the others, I rose to my feet. Resolving to find my strength, I wiped my cheeks with the back of my hands and turned toward my friends.

Jaid was pressed up against the bars, waiting for me. "I am sorry about your father."

"Me too," I answered in a low voice.

Before Jaid could could say anything else, Manny pressed his face as close to the bars as possible. "I'm sorry too. But if you're able, can you tell us what happened to you and Julio? Where is he?"

I gazed down at my tattered, blood-stained gown and filthy slippers. "My stab wound was healed in the Green Falls. When we returned to the palace, Maid Rell came out to us. She told us what had happened in the Great Hall after we left. Then she gave us a shimmer so we could escape Faevenly and the wrath of Malena and come back with reinforcements, but

Malena killed Maid Rell and closed the shimmer before I could get through."

"Does that mean Julio is in the human realm?" Leto asked, standing next to Jaid. "Did he get through?"

I narrowed my eyes at Leo. He looked a lot like Jaid —long silver hair, bright lavender eyes. The only real difference was that Leto looked older.

Jaid caught on to my stare right away. "We are brothers."

"Brothers?" I gazed at Jaid, my childhood friend, wondering what else I did not know about him.

"Yes, brothers. It was best no one knew."

Leto brought my attention back to his question. "Is Julio in the human realm?"

"He is. He went through the shimmer before it was destroyed."

Manny let out a sigh of relief. "Thank you, Jesus. He'll get help and come get us." Nobody responded. "Um, right?" he asked with a nervous chuckle. He nudged Leto. "Right?"

Leto placed his finger over his lips, letting us know there could be guards nearby listening. "Time will tell." He moved to the back of the cage. Ferna, Parlan, and Manny joined him.

I kept close to the bars, realizing I had been holding onto them for dear life. I loosened my grip but stayed where I was so I could see Jaid.

"Jaid," I said in a low voice. "I am sorry I doubted you."

His face softened. "Do not be sorry. I am the one

who owes you an apology for not telling you about my true allegiance. But we thought it best to protect you."

"I understand."

We stayed like that for a bit, when the dagger and the satchel of sleeping powder sprang to mind. I motioned at him, pointed to my thigh, and then ran a finger across my throat. He straightened his stance, catching on right away that I had a weapon. He went over to Leto and the others and started whispering.

While they strategized, I made my way around the perimeter of my small cage. A lone bucket took up the space in the corner, and that was it. I went back to the bars and scanned the open space and the corridor as best as I could. If someone sat nearby lurking, they were either incredibly quiet or too far away to be heard. Either way, we needed to be careful with our words.

Jaid, Leto, and Manny came to the bars. Behind them, Ferna and Parlan started bickering.

"You stepped on my toe, Ferna!" Parlan yelled.

"Well, you were in my way!" Ferna exploded.

They continued with their fiery exchange while Jaid spoke in the lowest of tones, so that I had to study his lips to understand him.

"What do you have?" he asked, pointing at my dress.

With Ferna and Parlan doing a magnificent job of drowning out our conversation, I answered, "A small dagger and a satchel of sleeping powder."

Leto quirked an eyebrow. "How much powder?"

"More than enough to get us out of here."

Leto rubbed his chin, then whispered. "We have been here only a day before you, but as far as we can tell, there is only one guard with a key. The one who escorted us in. If you can get the powder on him while he is letting you out of your cage, you can get the key and we can escape."

I pictured the guard in my mind. Tall, thin, long nose, with dark eyes and dark hair worn in a long braid. "Do the guards have a schedule?" I asked.

Jaid shook his head. "No. It seems there is much chaos happening in the village. Every now and again we hear scuffling. It could be the making of a rebellion, but we are not sure."

The fact that there was unrest was good for our cause. "And what of the Caileans? What happened to them?"

"They were executed yesterday," Jaid said.

My stomach plunged. "Oh, Malena," I muttered, hardly even believing she could have fallen into so much hatred. Or did she have that in her this whole time, and I had not noticed? I did not know. But my heart hurt for her.

"She is a murderer," Leto seethed. "Do not give her pity."

With my heart in my throat again, I forced my feelings to still. Leto was right. Malena was not the person I thought she was. Not at all. And even though there was no direct blood on her hands, she was most decidedly a murderer.

"You could not have known what was inside of her," Jaid added, sensing my turmoil. "It even surprises me."

Footsteps pounded the corridor, and a guard came to my cage. The one with the key. "Put the leather back in your mouth," he ordered.

The wad had fallen to the floor. I picked it up, wiped it off, and placed it back in my mouth.

"Place your hands behind your back and face the back of the wall."

I thought I could easily whip out my dagger and overtake him, but the voice of another guard stilled me.

"You want me to get the others?" he asked.

"No, only this one is wanted."

With my hands clasped behind me, I turned away from the bars and stood where he wanted. The lock clicked open, and the guard came in. He wrapped a rope around my wrists and tugged it in place. He jerked me around, then moved behind me and held a staff at my back.

"Move forward," he ordered.

After a quick glance at Jaid and the others, I stepped out of the cage and headed down the corridor. We emerged out in the open and the guard prodded me to the stairs and up to the dais. I averted my gaze, not wanting to take in the gruesome sight of my lifeless father, but found it impossible not to sneak a peek. Luckily, the area had been emptied and wiped clean. Even the crowd had dispersed.

"To the door," the guard instructed.

Two guards flanked the massive stone door. They swung it open as I neared. Once inside, I found myself in a huge open space. Oversized lit torches flanked the walls. Fresh air and bright sunlight poured in from a circular opening above me. And before me loomed a towering, yet simple stone carved throne. There were no etchings or grooves on the backrest or armrests. No seal of any sort. But it was big enough for the largest frame.

"Impressive in its simplicity, would you not say?" Draven asked. He stood cloaked in black and came forward from a shadowy spot in the corner of the room.

I straightened my back and raised my chin, refusing to show him any weakness.

Draven flicked his hand toward the guard. "Remove her gag."

The guard opened his hand in front of me. "Spit it out."

I did as he said but kept my silence as he walked away.

The witch lowered his hood and studied me with sparkling menacing eyes. "So proud you are, Celyse. Even with your human mother executed upon your birth and your father executed before your eyes, you still stand so tall. And such a shame about Maid Rell." He moved in close. "How do you manage such strength despite causing the deaths of so many? If not for you, they would be alive right now."

I hated that he was right but did not show any reaction. I refused to give him the satisfaction.

"Now, about Malena. I thought you might like to know that she asked me, very quickly I might add, for my assistance. She practically begged me to stand beside her. The princess has ambition. Or, I should say, the High Queen."

Malena had always wanted to be High Queen, but I never imagined it would be like this. Not in a thousand lifetimes could I have guessed it.

"Celyse, lovely Celyse." He trailed a finger down my cheek. "Do you not have anything to say about your half-sister?"

I continued holding my tongue, knowing he was only trying to incite me and refusing to give him the pleasure.

"Oh, I know what will get you talking," he said. "Do you want to know why you are still alive?"

Although the thought had crossed my mind, I did not think it wise to ask. Draven was as cunning as he was dangerous. I could not even imagine the evil that swirled in his head nor the trickery of words that were ready to flow from his mouth.

"I take your silence as a yes." He began circling me, his cape swishing with each step. "At first, the High Queen did not know what to do with you and your father. After much thought and consideration she decided to order both of you executed for your treacherous crimes with the shimmers. I thought it a wise decision for your father, but convinced her to wait on your sentence. Would you like to know why?" He paused for effect. "I will tell you why. I have no doubt your human is searching for a way back to you. No doubt at all. So, you see, you are my bait," he said with a click of his tongue. "When he comes here, I will end him. Unless, of course, I find him first. I almost found him yesterday in the human realm, in a city near his home."

Draven searched for Julio in the human realm? Fear and worry and anger exploded inside of me. As much as I did not want it to show, I could no longer hold my tongue. I swung my attention on him. "He bested you once, Draven. And I have no doubt he will do it again. Either in his realm or in this one."

Draven halted. His smug expression fell away. His eyes narrowed. "Julio Avila has no idea what I am capable of. And neither do you."

He flicked his cape behind him and walked off. "Take her back," he called out.

6

MALENA

An eerie hush smothered the palace as I sat on the window seat in my bedchamber. Staring at the twinkling stars and half-moon sky, I still could not believe the horror that had befallen me. Picking apart my life, I wondered how I never saw Celyse for who she really was. The way she sometimes carried on like a commoner, her weaknesses and whimsies. But more than that, how did I not see my Father's treachery? He most assuredly favored Celyse, and now I knew why.

But Father did not matter anymore. By now Draven had exacted punishment on him. Now my only concern was Celyse and her wretched band. I would need to handle them with haste, and I was more than eager to see the task done.

A flicker of movement in the shadows caught my eye. I gasped and clutched my throat. Was it Rook? Was he here to end me? Before I could call for Windon, the slow-moving form of my wolfbeasts came into view. I let out an exhale and eased my shoulders, grateful to have them roaming the grounds.

With Alexander handling things in the Sublands,

and the maid servants retired to their quarters, I had never felt more alone.

My thoughts drifted to Mother. I had not seen her since she had fallen undead and been placed in her bedchamber days ago. The maid servants and palace healer tended to her needs and reported to me on her status. Which, of course, had not changed. As an undead, she simply appeared to be sleeping—motionless and suspended in time. Was I ready to see her like that? And if I went to her, would she feel my presence? Hear my words?

I was not sure, but I had to take the chance. I needed her now more than ever.

Gathering my resolve, I forced myself away from the window and donned my silk robe and slippers, then stepped out into the corridor. Windon had urged me to allow him to serve as my constant guard, and he stood outside my door. He nodded when he saw me and followed me as I walked down the corridor of the wing I used to share with Celyse. I took the stairs up one flight to the regal floor where Father's private study, Mother's private sitting room, and their bedchamber were.

My pace slowed as I neared my destination, my unease growing steadily inside me. When I reached the oversized wooden door carved with intricate vines and blossoms, I halted. Celyse and I used to spend hours at this door, tracing the carvings with our fingers and telling stories of epic battles and romantic love stories. Now I was fighting an epic battle of my own, and Celyse and her band were the villains.

"Is all well, High Queen?" Windon asked from behind me.

With my courage restored, I straightened my posture, knowing Mother would expect nothing less than me assuming my rightful place. "All is well. Please make sure I am not disturbed."

He bowed. "Yes, High Queen."

I entered the room, closed the door behind me, and stayed in place while my eyes adjusted to the dim lighting from the orbs floating overhead. Ever so slowly, the raised canopy bed came into view, as did the still form of my mother on top.

With a gulp, I approached with slow steps, my eyes fixed on Mother's perfectly placed body. She wore a simple long white silk gown. Her hands were stacked one on top of the other on her waist, and her long silver tresses were combed straight.

"Mother." The word came out broken and shaky. I cleared my throat. "Mother. It is me, Malena."

I was not sure what I was expecting, but my heart sank when she gave no response. How foolish of me to think otherwise. I moved in closer, her sharp features striking even in her state. She had the ideal blend of intimidating beauty. Her exquisitely crafted face with high cheekbones, full lips, perfect nose, and mesmerizing eyes drew the attention of all who met her. But it was her sharp wit and biting tongue that kept everyone in place. There had never been a High Queen like her, and I hoped I could be half as great.

"I have been doing much in your absence, stepping into your role as best I can. Which is why I have not been here sooner."

It was not exactly why, but close enough. I did not want to admit any wrongdoing or let her know I feared visiting. She would not like that.

"Alexander and his family have been wonderful, supporting me and our house. I have also accepted his marriage request. We have decided, though, to put off the binding ceremony until House Strong and the realm are in order."

I studied her closed eyelids, expecting a twitch or a flutter, but did not get one.

"I go before the Council of Five soon for the official recognition of my status as High Queen. It will, of course, be forfeited once your condition is reversed. Draven is searching for a remedy for you." And then I mumbled in the lowest tone, "I do hope he finds one."

Her chest rose slowly, then fell so gradually I barely detected it.

"Father has been dealt with, executed for his wrongdoings. It was swift, and he did not suffer." My thoughts drifted to my half-sister, thinking it did not matter that we shared a father. A human was a human, in any degree. "As for Celyse, I wanted the same punishment exacted on her, but Draven wants to see if her human will come for her. If he does, they can both be dealt with at the same time. Until then, she has been banished to the Sublands, along with her traitorous group. I hope you approve."

I studied her long and slender hands, then looked down at mine. They were identical in every way.

"There is much to be considered with the Sublands—who will rule now that the Caileans have revealed their traitorous nature. They too have been executed. As for the dreadful Rook, he somehow escaped death. We do not know where he is, but Draven has orders to find him and kill him."

Inching in slightly closer with each word, I found myself at the edge of her bed. I reached out and placed my hand on hers. Her warm skin surprised me, though I was not sure what I expected. She was still alive, after all.

"Mother, I had to take your place with Draven to get him to help me, which means I have assumed your bargain. I wish you could tell me what it is. He assures me he will tell me when it is time for me to know. I admit I am frightened, but then I tell myself that if you made the bargain, then it should be well for me."

I moved closer to her and traced her long fingers with mine, willing them to move. But they did not.

"I hope you are proud of me, Mother." I wrapped my fingers around hers. "I am trying my best to make choices you would approve and to be like you as much as possible."

The quiet of the room settled in around us as my heart ached for my mother's touch, her smile, her words . . . anything. I lowered myself onto the mattress, careful not to disturb her, and sat next to her in silence for a while.

"The guard detail assures me of their loyalty. But I do fear another upheaval. Lesser beings always want to take down those in power, right, Mother?"

A soft knock sounded on the door. I set Mother's hand back on top of her other one, then rose to my feet.

"Come in," I said, my voice sounding too loud in the quiet room.

With Maid Rell gone, I had needed a new head maid servant and handed the duty to Maid Gidna. She was a young dwarf with short-cropped red hair, a face full of freckles, and an unusually soft voice. She cracked open the door and poked her head in.

"High Queen, I apologize for the disturbance, but a message has arrived from Alexander."

I held out my hand. "Give it to me."

She entered and took quick steps my way. She placed a small scroll on my palm. "Do you require anything else, High Queen?" Her gaze flicked to Mother for a quick second before returning to me. Other than the palace healer, not many had seen my mother in her state.

"Only privacy."

She curtsied. "Yes, High Queen."

Unrolling the parchment, I went back to Mother's bed, waited for Gidna to leave, and read out loud. "My Dearest Malena. I have left the Sublands and am now back home in High Meadow. I left Draven in charge, as per your request, and Celyse and her traitorous group remain caged. Upon my arrival home, I received word of grumblings amongst the other provinces. It seems Cuesta and perhaps Summit Range aim to oppose your being named High Queen at the meeting of the Council of Five."

I flung my hands down at my sides and looked at Mother with a huff. "Did you hear that? Those traitorous fools," I seethed. "They do not know what I am capable of. But they will see, Mother. They will see."

Steadying myself, I continued reading. "My father and I leave for Cuesta tomorrow to investigate. I shall keep you informed. All my love, Alexander."

The idea of Cuesta and Summit Range working against me made my blood boil. My mind locked on Jorn Lind. He was from Cuesta. He had tried to harm Celyse, and as a result, was killed on palace grounds. Now it seemed they wanted retribution for the loss of their son after all, even though Lord Lind had indicated remorse over their son's actions.

And it was all because of Celyse.

"Celyse is doing it again!" I spat, clutching the parchment and crumpling it in my fist. "She ruined my courtship season, the reputation of House Strong, and now she is ruining my crown. I will not have it, Mother!"

If Mother were alive, what would she say? What would she do? I closed my eyes, struggling to find the perfect answer, rage building inside of me with each passing moment, when I heard a soft whisper.

"End her."

My eyes snapped open. An icy chill traveled down my body. My gaze landed on my mother. She lay in the exact same position—eyes closed; lips shut. Not even her hands had moved. But without a doubt, it was her voice I had heard.

I crept toward her. "Mother?" I reached out to touch her hand. "Did you say something?"

The door opened, and I spun around with a start.

"High Queen," gaped the palace healer, Lady Sonia. She wore a pale blue dress, and her dark hair flowed loose down her back. She carried a towel in one hand and a jar of green healing cream in the other. She bowed low. "I was not expecting you. My apologies. I will come back another time."

"No," I said, stopping her from leaving. "I am finished here."

"Very well," she said.

Sonia had served the Strongs for as long as I could remember. She knew my mother as well as anyone. Looking from her to my mother's body, I wondered if she had heard whisperings during her visits.

"Lady Sonia," I said, pausing while my mind crafted the best way to ask my question. "You tend to my mother every evening, correct?"

"Yes, I do." She raised the jar. "I apply healing cream to her feet, legs, and arms. It is my hope the cream will help revive her. It is made from sage, calendula, and algae, mixed with healing waters from the Green Falls. I also speak to her."

I raised a brow. "You speak to her?"

"Yes."

"What do you say?"

"I say prayers and affirmations, High Queen. The spoken word is powerful."

"That is most admirable. I appreciate your efforts." I thumbed the wadded parchment in my hand. "Does she . . . ever speak back?"

Lady Sonia blinked. "No. She is undead."

"Of course," I replied quickly. "It was a silly question." Swishing the train of my robe behind me, I said, "I will leave you to your duty. Good night, Lady Sonia."

Lady Sonia bowed her head. "Good night, High Queen."

As I made my way back to my bedchamber, my mother's whisper swirled in my head. I had no idea how she had been able to communicate with me, and truly, it did not matter. If Mother wanted me to end Celyse, then I would end her. But what of Draven? He wanted to keep Celyse around to trap Julio. But was that the best course of action for me? Had I done the right thing by assuming my mother's role with him?

Back in my bedchamber, I went to my desk. I held Alexander's note over a small glass jar and lit it from the nearby candle. It burst into a small flame, and I dropped it in the glass.

"I am the High Queen," I muttered. "No one is as important as me. Not even Draven the witch."

7
JULIO

With the reality of school and work obligations setting in, the number of family members in the house dwindled over the next few days until it was only me, my mom, and my cousin Trent who didn't have to go back to college right away. With *Tia* Maria and *Tio* Tony working and their three kids in school, Mom, Trent, and I got busy strategizing.

Mom found a notebook and started writing everything out. "First, we know that the fae realm overlays the human realm," she wrote.

"Yes," I held out my hands with one hovering over the other, thinking of Manny's Oreo comparison. "There's a thing called the stratus in the middle."

Mom studied my hands. "I see." She continued writing, then looked up at me. "As for the good guys," she continued, "there's, of course, our Manny, and then Celyse, Leto, and who else?"

"Ferna, Parlan, and Jaid. There may be others. But that's who Manny is with."

Mom wrote down the names. "And who are the evil ones?"

"Draven and Malena. I'm sure they've got others working with them, but I have no idea who they are."

"Draven and Malena—those just sound evil," Trent added.

"You don't even know," I muttered.

Mom tapped the pen against her chin and studied her notes, her lips moving as if reading to herself. She pointed at the word *stratus*. "What is this exactly, *mijo*?"

"Well, the stratus is where the shimmery portals come from."

"Shimmery portals?" Trent asked.

I cupped my hands and brought them together, as if holding an invisible ball. "They're opaque round bubble-looking things that you can stretch out and use to cross back and forth between the realms by stepping through." I pulled my hands apart to show her. "Like magical doorways."

"*Muy interesante*," she mumbled. She wrote the word *shimmer* and circled it.

"Well, we need a shimmer, then," Trent said in a hopeful tone, as if finding one was easy to do.

I rubbed the back of my neck. "Only fae have shimmers. And the fae that lived in Austin, Leto, had his house burned down by Draven." I scooted up to the edge of my seat as I thought of something. "Wait a minute. I remember him storing Celyse's shimmer somewhere on his property. Maybe his backyard."

"Good," Mom said. She wrote *Leto's casa* on her paper. She looked at me and asked, "Anywhere else?"

"Actually, yeah. Leto's friends Ferna and Parlan

have a bakery. Maybe we can find something over there."

"Bakery," she said. She wrote the word, set her pencil down, and sat back. Crossing her arms, she studied everything she had written, her gaze sweeping across the paper until it locked on one word—Draven.

"Mom, what is it?"

With a trembling hand, she reached her fingers out and brushed her fingertips over Draven's name. "Draven is evil like the devil."

Her words came out more like a statement and less like a question. I swallowed, picturing the dark-cloaked witch perfectly in my mind. "Yeah, he is like the devil."

She rubbed her forehead, her expression filled with worry and dread. "We cannot stay at *Tio* Tony's house. It's too dangerous. We cannot risk something happening to them."

"Wait a minute. Do you sense they're in danger?" Trent asked, his eyes widening with fear.

She shook her head slightly. "I am not sure. But I would rather be safe than sorry."

Mom was right. I would never forgive myself if something happened to *Tio* Tony, *Tia* Maria, or the kids. I had already jeopardized Manny, and there was no way I'd let anything happen to them too. Or anyone else for that matter. We needed to leave.

"Where will we go?" I asked, staring at the refrigerator door filled with their pictures, school papers, and little kid drawings, thinking of their normal lives and how mine used to be normal. "Where is safe?"

"Y'all can come to Houston," Trent offered. "My mom, grandma, and I aren't afraid of evil."

Mom smiled, and patted Trent's arm. "Thank you, *mijo*. I know you all are not afraid. But I have an idea of where we can go. You too, if you want to join us, but you don't have to. I only need to talk to Sister Catherine first."

"I'm definitely in," Trent replied. "No way am I leaving the two of you to deal with this."

I clapped Trent on the back, grateful to have him with me, then said to my mom, "Sister Catherine that gave you a ride to your church retreat a few days ago?"

"Yes. The nuns have a few retreat houses in the Austin area. I'm pretty sure they will let us use one."

Mom retrieved her phone from the kitchen counter and called Sister Catherine. She explained how we needed a place to stay while our house underwent repairs. Like Mom thought, Sister Catherine was quick to say yes, offering us their retreat home in Dripping Springs, which wasn't too far. With that out of the way, we gathered our things and called *Tio* Tony to tell him we were leaving. He said he understood, and for us to call if we needed anything. Then we took off.

As I drove, my thoughts filled with the chaos that had occurred at my house—Draven appearing and hurling his red energy like bombs; Leto, Ferna, and Parlan showing up with arrows drawn; Leto opening a shimmer and all of us jumping through.

I wondered what my house looked like now.

"Hey, Mom," I said. "Mind if I drive by the house on the way? I want to see it."

After a long pause, she nodded. "Okay."

When my parents were young and before they had me, my dad worked long, hard hours as a car repairman and my mom cooked in the kitchen of a small Mexican food restaurant. They did that for years, living on a tight budget, and saved their money until they could afford to buy a house. About a year before I was born, they finally had enough in the bank to make their dreams a reality.

They bought a house and moved in with hand-me-down furniture. They put their personal stamp on the house by painting the rooms yellow—the color of sunshine—and, of course, filling the house with love and laughter and delicious food.

Mom always said our home was magical—that she and my dad were so happy there raising me. But then my dad disappeared, and everything changed. And now, it had changed even more because of Draven.

I dreaded seeing what he had done.

I turned into my neighborhood and slowed down as I drove down my street. I kept my stare on the white lines on the road before slowly bringing my gaze to my house.

The sight gutted me.

My once pristine, small red-brick home with black trim resembled a home wrecked by a fiery tornado. Plywood covered the area where our front door and front windows used to be. Streaks of black charred the brick in all directions, as if it had been bombarded by a lightning storm. The once lush and green front yard looked trampled and brown. The massive oak tree in the front Manny and I used to climb as kids was split in two.

"Oh, Mom," I muttered, as my vision blurred over.

"I know," Mom said in a low voice. She placed her hand on my shoulder and squeezed. It was the kind of squeeze she gave to let me know everything was going to be okay. I didn't exactly believe it would be but held on to her faith anyway. She always had enough faith for the both of us.

"Sorry, *primo*," Trent offered from the backseat.

"I didn't think it'd be that bad." I rubbed my eyes and parked the car in the front. The ghostly couple that roamed our street came into view. They were arm in arm, strolling as usual. They stared at me suspiciously but walked past the car without saying anything.

"Mr. and Mrs. Trevino," I muttered. "They were there when Draven came. They tried to help me, as well as a ghost girl with white hair—Abigail."

"A ghost girl?" Mom said. "I haven't seen a ghost girl, but the Trevinos came to me after you and Manny disappeared and told me what happened. Because of them, I didn't file a missing persons report. Neither did Manny's father. We knew the police couldn't help us find you."

"How did you explain the damage, then?" I asked.

"The cops and the fire department must've showed up with lots of questions."

"They did. But I didn't have to explain anything since I wasn't here. Several neighbors reported seeing a man in a black cloak shooting at the house with what they claimed was a blaster of some sort, and that he charged into the house and then disappeared."

I rubbed my face. "Sounds about right."

After a bit, Mom asked, "Do you need anything from the house, *mijo*? Even though the front is damaged, the back of the house and our bedrooms were spared."

"Nah," I said, trying to shake off the guilt over everything that had happened because of me. "The stuff you packed for me is fine."

I drove away from the house and started heading for Dripping Springs. After a long stretch of silence, my mom, Trent, and I arrived at the church retreat house. Mom took the biggest room overlooking the back garden, and Trent and I set up our stuff in a bunk room next to hers. Not that we had much stuff.

"When do we go to this guy Leto's house?" asked Trent.

"Now," I said, eager for action.

We went to Mom's room and found her sitting on the edge of the bed, gazing out the window. She was so lost in her thoughts, she didn't even hear us walk in.

"Mom, we're gonna head out now," I said.

She kept her attention on the trees. "Before you

leave, I want to try something." Her brows were stitched together, her face hardened, and her shoulders were slightly raised and pulled in. I kept quiet while her ideas percolated. Even Trent didn't say anything.

"What is it?" I asked.

She blew out, then rubbed her hands together. "I think I can send your spirit to her, *mijo*."

Her words surprised me. "You can send my spirit . . . to Celyse in Faevenly?"

She nodded. "If I can bring spirits over to talk to the living, then I should be able to send the living to talk to a spirit."

"But she's not a spirit, Mom," I said, shaking my head. "She's alive."

"I know, *mijo*. But it's the same idea. If you can focus your thoughts on Celyse with precision and clarity, then I think I can send you to her."

Trent gulped and shifted his stance. "*Tia*, you've done that before?"

"Many times. That's how I help my clients communicate with their loved ones who've passed on. I sometimes even let them inhabit my body for a short while. But I have never done it with another realm like Faerie."

"Mom," I said, my heart swelling with the possibility of seeing Celyse. "If you think you can do it, then we need to try. I need to know if she is okay. Manny too. She might even be able to give us information on how we can save them."

She rubbed her hands on her pants and nodded. "I

agree, *mijo*." She rose to her feet and motioned for us to follow her. "Come, let us go to the kitchen."

The large house had an expansive kitchen with dark wood floors, green walls, brown cabinets, and stainless-steel appliances. A huge portrait of Jesus and his disciples at the Last Supper hung on the wall over the large rectangular table. A floor-to-ceiling display of crosses covered another wall.

It was your typical Catholic kitchen, but on steroids.

We took our seats with me facing my mom. She made the sign of the cross up and down her body and then shoulder to shoulder, the way she did before every session. Trent and I did the same. She held out her small hands and I scooped them into mine. She spoke in a calm tone.

"Julio, I want you to close your eyes and relax. Take deep breaths. Slow your heart and let go of any tension in your body. When you are completely at ease, I want you to visualize Celyse."

"Okay," I mumbled. Shutting my eyes, I did what she said, and it didn't take long for the image of Celyse to form in my mind—long silver hair with a streak of black, full pink lips, majestic emerald eyes that sparkled like precious gems. Soft skin and hair that smelled like a bouquet of flowers. The image of her was so clear, I could almost feel her presence.

"*Mijo*, do you see her?"

"I see her."

"Good. Now, go to her."

"Go to her?"

"Yes. Move toward her as if you two are in the same space. I will work to project your energy. When you feel as if you can touch her, I want you to open your eyes."

I blew out and shifted in my seat. "Okay."

I thought I knew what it meant to project energy onto someone, but I had no idea how something like that would work with someone in a different realm. But if Mom said she could do it, then she could do it.

Pushing my uncertainties aside, I continued focusing on Celyse. In a blink, the image of her wasn't in mind any more. Instead, she was straight ahead, standing in a dark room, facing away from me. The space all around blurred, then shifted into focus. I shuffled toward her. I stretched out my hand. Before I touched her shoulder, I opened my eyes.

With a start, she turned around, her silver hair swaying with her movement, her eyes widening with surprise.

"Julio!"

"Celyse!"

We rushed each other, our arms whooshing through each other's bodies.

She gasped. "You are a spirit? Are you"—tears flooded her eyes as her words cut short— "no longer alive?"

"No, I'm not a spirit. I'm alive and well. I'm in the human realm. My mom is helping me project myself over here."

She placed her hands on her chest and let out an exhale. “Thank the sun, moon and stars. I have been so worried.”

“Me too. When I stepped through the shimmer and you weren’t behind me, I didn’t know what happened.”

She still wore her gold wedding dress with a splotch of blood on it. It was tattered and dirty, looking as if it’d been dragged through the mud. Her normally shiny and smooth hair hung in a state of disarray. Scanning the area, I spotted bars with a dirt floor and cave walls. A prison cell?

I reached for her hand, but my fingers passed right through her. “Where are you? What’s happened? And is Manny okay?”

“He is fine. But, matters are most dire. Malena killed Maid Rell after you stepped through the portal. Now I am imprisoned. So are Manny, Leto, Ferna, Parlan, and Jaid. We are in the Sublands and they are on the other side of an underground prison. Malena and Alexander have stepped into the roles of High Queen and High King, and they have formed an alliance with Draven.”

“Oh no,” I muttered, my mind reeling.

“It is worse than that. Malena has gone mad. She ordered the execution of the Caileans.” She stopped and swallowed while tears flooded her eyes. “And my father, too.”

“Oh, Celyse. I’m so sorry.” I reached out to touch her face, my shimmery hand hovering inches away from her cheek. “But thank God you’re okay.”

"Thanking a god will not help any of us. Draven and Malena want you dead. The mad witch searches for you in both realms. I am only alive because he is using me as bait should you find a way to cross back over." Pain etched across her face, and she tried to grab my hands. "I cannot lose you."

Her vulnerability tugged at my heart, sending my emotions all over the place. "You're not going to lose me."

We moved closer to each other, pulled together by the love we shared. "What are we to do? How can we even get out of this?" she asked.

My brain zeroed in on the fact that she was with Leto. "First thing we need to do is be together. For that to happen, I need a shimmer. Ask Leto where I can find one. Quick."

A spark of hope lit up her eyes. "Yes! He will know!" She moved to the bars to ask him when my vision dimmed. My head blared with pain, nearly sending me to my knees.

"Julio!" she cried out.

The image of her blurred away and was replaced with the face of my mom shaking me awake. "*¡Necesitamos ir!*"

Trent grabbed my arm and pulled me from my seat. "Come on!"

Tumbling out of my chair, I barely caught my footing as we raced out of the house.

"What the hell is happening!?" I yelled.

"*Mal!*" Mom shouted as she ran.

Evil? Her warning chilled me to the bone. Whatever she had felt was Draven; I knew it.

Trent fumbled with his keys as we darted to his car. We hopped in, and he cranked the ignition. Slamming his foot against the accelerator, he zoomed out of the driveway and peeled down the street.

We were almost out of the neighborhood when my mom called out, "Okay, *ya*!" She was near breathless, panting as she clutched the cross hanging around her neck. "It has passed."

Trent slowed his driving and pulled over to the side of the road. He threw the car in park and rested his head back. "What in the hell," he muttered.

Sitting next to my mom in the backseat, I grabbed her hand and squeezed. "Are you okay?"

"Yes, *gracias a Díos*. I am okay." She swallowed, steadying her breathing. "I felt something in the space around us when you were in the other realm. Or maybe it was in the fae realm. I could not tell."

"Something like what?" Trent asked.

"Like Draven," I muttered.

Mom nodded. "Something dark and evil."

A shiver passed through me as I stared out the window, thinking of what Celyse had said. In this realm or in hers, I was at risk. "He's hunting me," I muttered.

"What do we do?" Trent asked.

"We stick to the plan," I said quickly. "No matter what. Celyse and Manny are counting on us."

Mom nodded. "I agree. I will stay at the house and

prepare things on my end. I will protect myself, you, and Trent as best I can while you search for the shimmer."

"Maybe you should come with us," I said. "Maybe we shouldn't be separated."

"Nonsense. The Lord is bigger than any evil. I will be fine."

If it were anyone else, I'd argue. But it was my mom, the most powerful *curandera* in Texas. People traveled from all over to see her. I had no doubt she'd be okay.

Trent and I took my mom back to the house. After a quick walk through, she said the house was clear, that whatever she had felt was gone. And then she shooed us away. She wanted us to get to Leto's before it got too late.

Loaded with flashlights, Trent and I set off. If a shimmer lay hidden somewhere on his property, I knew I could find it. I just hoped I wouldn't find it too late.

Hold on, babe, I thought to myself. *I'm coming*.

8
CELYSE

"Julio!" I called out in a hushed whisper, swiping my hand through the space where only moments before, his face had appeared. My heart lurched from fear. "Julio!"

"What?" Manny uttered, scrambling to his feet. He gripped the bars of his cage, then pressed his face forward. "Celyse, did you say Julio?"

"Yes." I moved about the space, waving my arms back and forth, hoping he would come back. "He was right here, but now he is gone."

"There in your cell?" Manny asked.

I turned to face Manny. "Yes. Right here. He came to me in spirit form. He said he is looking for a shimmer in the human realm so he can come for us. He wanted me to ask Leto where he could find one, but then he vanished."

Leto, Jaid, and the others rose to their feet and joined Manny at the bars. Leto glanced up and down the corridor, then said in a hushed voice, "It seems our witch is figuring things out. I have no doubt he will go to my property and find one, as I have a few hidden there."

"But your place burned to the ground," Manny said.

"It did. But the shimmers I have stored there are not in my house. I trust Julio will figure that out."

Footsteps pounded down the corridor, forcing everyone to quiet. A guard came into view, and behind him two others, dragging the body of a fae with long dark loose hair, dressed in the customary green pants and black shirts of Strong guards. The guards unlocked a cage farther down the corridor, tossed in the body with a thud, and then locked the door again. They marched away without a word.

When the silence returned, Manny asked, "Uh, do y'all know that guy?"

"It is hard to say," Jaid answered. "I could not see his face."

I patted my knife and my pouch of sleeping powders. "It makes no difference. We need to get out of here now. I am going to call a guard over and use my powder."

"But I have a key," a voice whispered.

My gaze met Jaid's before we looked in the direction the fae prisoner had been dragged. A lock clinked, and a door squeaked open. Two seconds later, the fae appeared before me. He had long dark hair and young blue eyes, and I was sure I had not seen him before.

He opened my lock. When the bars swung open, I clutched his throat with one hand, drew out my dagger with the other, and pressed the tip at his jugular.

"You are not a Strong guard," I hissed.

"No, I am not. But I stood with them, and you. I assure you." His throat bobbed against my hold. "I am on your side."

I removed my grip from his throat but kept my dagger steady. I held out my hand before him. "Give me the key."

"I am a Cailean guard. My name is Leaf. I was standing with the Strong guards at the wedding under orders from Rook. That is why I am wearing this garb. We were ordered to keep a uniform look."

"The key," I demanded.

His unflinching eyes stayed on me as he dropped the key onto my palm. I nudged him to the far end of the cage and locked him in, then went to Jaid's cage and let them out.

"I fought alongside all of you," Leaf declared, standing at the bars. "But I was not near the dais. I stood at the far side of the Great Hall, which is why you do not recognize me."

Jaid moved in and studied the fae. "Rook indeed brought a detail wearing similar attire. But after we were overtaken in the Great Hall, we were rounded up. While there, I studied each face. Yours was not amongst them."

"Besides, Rook is dead, and so are the Caileans," I added.

"I know very well they are dead. You do not need to tell me," Leaf said in a biting tone. "As for the Great Hall, you did not see me because I was ordered by Rook to escape and return here to protect the Caileans if something were to go awry. After the princess was wounded and taken, and Rook was killed, I did as ordered and snuck away." His face hardened and his jaw clenched. "I regret not making it here in time to save the Caileans. But when I saw you all being brought down here to the cages, I figured I could at least save your group."

Leto raised his brow slightly at Jaid and then me. "If he is a Sublander, he may be able to help us get out of here. They did fight with us, after all."

"He may also lead us to certain death. There were plenty of Sublanders cheering when we were out on that dais and my father lost his life," I countered. "And then who will be the fool?"

"You have my word on the sun, moon and stars that I will not hurt any one of you," Leaf offered. "On my honor."

"Honor is cheap these days," Ferna hissed.

Footsteps sounded in the distance. Manny's eyes flicked about nervously. "If someone is heading our way, then I say we trust the dude for now and let him lead us out of here."

"And if he should cross us, we kill him," Parlan tacked on. "He is outnumbered, after all."

Manny and Parlan had a point. Trust now, kill later. The reasoning made sense. I unlocked the door and moved aside. "Out."

Leaf bowed his head and stepped forward. "Thank you, my lady," he said in a less than grateful tone. "Now please, follow me."

He took a torch from the wall. Jaid took a torch too, and directed us into formation. "Leto behind the Sublander, then myself, Celyse, Manny, Ferna, and Parlan. Protect the princess."

"And the human." Manny said with a nervous laugh, his eyes so wide I thought they might pop. "I'm not exactly built for this kinda stuff."

I placed my hand on Manny's shoulder. It could not be easy being stuck in a foreign land, especially as a mere human. And to be a prisoner, no less. "You will be fine, Manny."

He drew in a deep breath, and I could feel his shoulder relax some. "Okay, yeah. You're right. I'm going to be fine. Thanks, Celyse."

We moved into place, ready to follow Leaf, when the young fae turned to face us. "Hold on, I need to get my things."

He made his way back to the entrance of the underground cages, returning swiftly with a satchel draped over his shoulder. We shot him incredulous stares.

"You all want to get any of your things?" he asked us.

"Young and foolish," Leto muttered. "But yes, we would like to have our weapons."

Leto made a move in the same direction as Leaf, but voices drifting from the entrance halted his advancement. "I guess we will not have our weapons after all."

With the voices growing louder, I prodded, "We need to go. Hurry."

The young fae took off at a quick pace and we followed. Soon, the voices drifted away and the only sounds that could be heard were our footsteps against the cave floor.

Staying in line, with humidity thickening around us, I could not stop thinking about Leaf. I did not know if he could be trusted. Even though his story made sense, fae were clever and could twist words with ease. I wondered if his were true or laced with deceit.

Traveling down the corridor, we did not pass any other cages. In fact, we did not pass any sign of civilization at all. Our cages must have been a special holding area. I wondered where the other cages were, especially since I knew that somewhere around here were enslaved humans.

The winding path narrowed in some places and widened in others. As it moved in a downward trajectory, the air began shifting from warm and humid to cool and damp. The change triggered a warning in me, and I began to feel as if something was amiss. Inching my hand under the ripped skirt of my dress, I found the hilt of my dagger and eased it out as we walked.

Manny got up close. "What are you doing?" he whispered.

"Getting ready," I said.

His mouthed dangled open for a second before he gulped. "For what?"

"For anything," I said in a low tone.

I motioned for him to be quiet and kept my focus on Jaid and Leto in front of me. Their gait had slowed, increasing the distance between themselves and Leaf. Jaid flexed and balled his hands at his sides, and I thought I detected a clench at his jaw. Whatever was happening, he felt it too.

"Leaf," Jaid said. "How much farther?"

"We have to go down before we go back up," the young fae said.

"How far down?" Leto asked, his tone laced with suspicion.

Leaf's step hesitated ever so slightly. "Only a bit more."

Leto stopped and held up his hand, prompting us to halt. Jaid moved next to his brother, and the pair closed in on Leaf.

"You had better explain what you are up to before I take your life from you," Jaid warned.

Leaf turned and assessed Jaid and Leto—his blue eyes dangerous and calculating. "I am leading you out of here, like I said I would, but first we are getting some aquoise."

"You are a thief!" Ferna accused.

"I am whatever I need to be to survive," Leaf spat.

I moved between Jaid and Leto and held out my dagger. "Why do you need it, and why not get it yourself?"

He glowered at me. "You have no right to question me. You are half human, enamored with a full human, and will leave this realm as soon as you can without giving a care to the fae or the humans enslaved here who do the Strongs' bidding."

Stunned at his accusation, my first reaction was to take his life myself. But then his words started sinking in, sending a hint of guilt swirling in my gut. "You know nothing, stranger."

"It makes no matter what I know. When you leave, Faevenly will fall under the rule of Malena with House Kane at her side and Draven the witch doing her bidding. The realm will be way worse than it ever was under your father and fake mother. My loyalists will need the aquoise if we are to have any chance of overthrowing Malena. It is our only hope."

I lowered my dagger. I never thought of my leaving as abandoning Faevenly, never imagined what would become of those I would leave behind—Jaid, Leto, Ferna, and Parlan, even Adva and Aedon. They were good and true and deserved to live in a peaceful and prosperous realm. Could they ever do that with Malena and Alexander ruling? Not to mention the innocent humans being taken through the shimmers.

"What do you propose, then?" I asked.

"You and your band will help me get as much aquoise as we can. And if you have any sense of right and wrong, you will help me kill Malena. Once she is out of the way, you can go wherever you wish. With the both of you gone, the Strong line of succession will no longer exist. Alexander Kane's aspirations to the throne will be derailed, and a more peaceful house can finally rule."

Kill Malena?

Malena was the one taking lives. Not me. Plus, I did not know if I could do it. She was my sister and used to be my best friend. We did everything together—play, study, travel, dream. There had to be some good in her. But what if there was none? She was born of a wicked mother after all.

Jaid must have seen the conflict in my face and was quick to reply for me. "You are in no position to make any requests," he threatened Leaf.

Leaf refused to back down to Jaid and the pair launched into a heated exchange while my thoughts stayed on Malena. She had joined Draven, a figure who had been like a monster to us for all our lives. Together they had killed our father and imprisoned me with the plan of using me to bait Julio. But what was her endgame with me? What was she planning for me in the long run? I had to believe she aimed to punish me for my crimes, the way she had punished my father. Draven had said so himself. It would do me and my allies well to have some aquoise and join Leaf's plan. At least until we could figure something else out.

"We will help you get aquoise," I announced, my words halting Leaf and Jaid seconds before throwing blows. "Some for you, and some for us, and you will get us safely out of the Sublands."

"And you will help me kill Malena?" Leaf asked.

I nodded. "We will help you."

Leaf nodded to me. "See? That was not so hard."

I jabbed my dagger at him. “Do not force me to change my mind.”

He smirked. “I would not even consider it.”

We followed him further down the winding path for a good while, when Leaf called out over his shoulder. “There is a turn up here to the right where the path becomes narrow and then steep for a bit. It will level out and become a flat surface.”

Just like he said, we turned and found ourselves in a narrow corridor. Moving sideways, we shuffled onward. After a few paces, the path angled sharply upward. After we had trudged like that for a bit, the angle leveled out, forming into a wide-open flat area with a low ceiling. Studying the cave walls in the light of our torches, I spotted blue flecks.

“Aquoise,” I murmured.

“It is everywhere,” Ferna marveled.

Leaf set his torch on a hook on the cave wall, then opened the satchel slung around his shoulder. He brought out three small pickaxes. “Get only the biggest pieces, and fast. These caves are not safe.”

Manny’s eyes grew wide as he glanced around. “Uh . . . did you just say *not* safe?”

“Yes, that is what I said. No one speaks of the terrors of the cave; but they, along with the dangers of mining, are why the Strongs began taking humans to perform the excavating.”

Jaid grabbed Leaf by the neck. “You said nothing of dangers.”

“You did not ask,” he shrugged.

Jaid tightened his grip, then released Leaf with a shove. "We get a few pieces and then we are out of here."

"Exactly my plan," Leaf said.

Jaid handed his torch to Ferna, and he, Leto, and Leaf started chipping away at the rock while I got to work with my dagger. "Is that why no one is down here?" I asked. "Because of the terrors?"

"Yes," Leaf admitted. "As you can see from the hooks along the walls, the excavation for aquoise extended this far, and even farther. But when the winds came, operations were moved closer to the surface to allow the guards a quick exit. But all the big chunks have been mined already. Only these smaller pieces remain. It is said that the supply is almost depleted."

"And where are all the mined pieces stored?" Leto asked.

"Under lock and key in the Sublands Keep," Leaf said. "Only the Strongs and their agents are allowed inside."

"And the humans?" Manny asked. "Where are they?"

"They have been moved, but I know not where," Leaf answered.

Placing the tip of the dagger at the edge of one of the blue flecks, I slammed my palm against the handle, my mind grappling with the clandestine operations of my father and the High Queen. Working the blade, a chunk of blue the size of a thumbnail broke free.

"Manny," I called out. "Put this in your pocket."

I tossed it to him and started on another fleck when a howling wind blasted all around us. Everyone froze.

"The cave terrors," Leaf warned. "Quick, everyone huddle together."

"Thunderation," Jaid muttered,

Everyone moved in, shuffling the pickaxes back in the bag. Manny pressed up beside me. "I'm kinda freaking right now."

"Stay calm," I said. "And close."

Another blast of air whooshed by. This time it stayed and circled us like a whirlwind. A howling came with it, like a menacing warning. It grew louder with each passing second. But the words were foreign, and I could not make them out.

"W-w-we need to get out of here. R-r-right the h-h-hell now," Manny whispered in a trembling voice.

Leaf slung his bag over his shoulder and grabbed his torch. "This way." Then he yelled over his shoulder. "And whatever you do, do not look down at the ground."

"Why?" I called out, angry over the dangers Leaf had not told us about. "What is on the ground?"

"Deadly magic," Leaf said.

"W-w-what?" Manny asked.

We lined up the way we had come in and scurried off the plateau and down the steep slope, then twisted and turned in the opposite direction we had come from. We weaved our way up and down, following Leaf's bobbing torch light, but we could not escape the wind. It stayed with us, filling our ears and reverberating through our heads.

This time, I heard the wind's repeating message. "Look down. Look down. Look down."

The voice tugged at me with a force, almost pulling my will into compliance.

"Y-y-y'all, I want to look d-d-down!" Manny called out.

"Do not!" Leto hollered.

"Okay, okay. Eyes up, eyes up, eyes up . . ." I heard Manny pleading with himself behind me.

"That is right, Manny. Eyes up!" I shouted.

Resisting the urge to glance at whatever was happening below our feet, I found myself repeating Manny's mantra in my head when suddenly Manny's chanting stopped, as did his movement. Ferna, and Parlan crashed into him like an accordion, sending him tumbling against my back.

I spun around to see his head pointed downward, his body eerily still. "Oh no." I lifted his chin. A blue haze clouded his brown eyes, like a film. My stomach sank.

"I've got him!" Leto scooped up Manny and slung him over his shoulder. "Go, Celyse!"

With Manny secured, I continued following Jaid in front of me and Leaf beyond, the howling so thick in my head I had to bite my lip so I would not look down.

After another turn, a soft ray of light came into view. It filtered from the side of the cave wall. We ran to it and skidded to a stop in front of a crevice.

"This way!" Leaf said, tossing his torch. He disappeared through the narrow opening, followed by Jaid and then me. Glancing over my shoulder, I saw Leto. He and Manny were cramming their way through. I was saying a silent prayer to the sun, moon and stars for them to make it when I realized something—the wind had stopped.

"Almost there!" Leaf called out.

The light grew brighter, the cave opening wider until we tumbled out into the brilliant sunlight. I shielded my eyes with my hands, holding them there until the splotches littering my sight disappeared. I looked down, now that I could. My gold wedding slippers were as dark as mud, and under my feet the ground was red dirt. There was no more magic.

"That was close," Ferna breathed out, leaning over with her hands on her knees.

Getting my bearings, I saw that we were not in the rock village anymore. We must have traversed far enough that we ended up on the back side, though I could not exactly tell. I was just glad we were out.

Leto walked over to a large boulder and set Manny down, leaning him against the rock. "Will he return to normal?" Leto asked Leaf.

"Yes," Leaf answered. "After a few hours."

Kneeling before Manny, I moved his thick curly hair away from his face and checked his forehead. My palm met perfectly cool skin, and I took that as a good sign.

"What happened to him?" I asked.

Leaf shrugged his shoulders. “He looked down.”

I glowered at the dark-haired fae. “Besides that.”

Leaf dusted off the sleeves of his shirt. “The cave terrors can do all sorts of things—including make others see things that are not there. But whatever is seen is different for each observer. For Manny, he saw something that literally scared him into a stupor.”

A shudder worked its way through me as I thought of what Manny must have seen. “Awful,” I whispered.

“Now what?” Jaid asked, walking the area. “There is nothing out here.”

Leaf pointed. “Beyond that ridge is a small village. They have an inn where we can clean up and get food and supplies. They will also have horses we can purchase.” He patted his pouch. “They will accept aquoise as payment.”

Leto lifted Manny back over his shoulder. “Let us go, then. I am certain our absence will be noticed soon if it has not already.”

We trooped through the barren land with the sun beating down on us, my mind sifting through what Leaf had said about Faevenly and Malena. He was right. If she were left to rule, the realm would suffer. I could not let that happen.

With my mind on Malena, the walk to the small village passed quickly. Before we got too close, Leaf halted.

“What is it?” Jaid asked.

“We cannot walk into the village with the princess

looking the way she does," he said. "We must conceal her."

"And your idea is?" Leto asked.

"Everyone should wait here while I secure an outfit for her," Leaf said. He glanced at Leto, who was still carrying Manny. "And maybe a cart with a blanket for the human."

I thought his plan a sound one, but did not trust the young fae at all. Leto thought the same. He set Manny on the ground. "Good idea. Ferna and Parlan will accompany you."

"Of course they will," Leaf grumbled.

With Leaf, Ferna, and Parlan on their way, I sat on the ground next to Manny. I scanned the desolate surroundings, thinking how not long ago I had been surrounded by opulence. "It is surreal to think how much our lives have changed in such a small amount of time."

"True. Not long ago, I was minding my own business, fishing off the pier at my lake house in the human realm without a care in the world," Leto mused. "Contemplating what to cook for dinner."

Jaid kept his stare keen, his feet wide. "This path we are on was predetermined years ago. You two are only now aware."

I laughed. "Fools, Leto. He is calling us fools."

Leto made a grand gesture toward his brother. "I am convinced that Jaid is the wisest of us all."

Staring at my childhood friend, remembering all the times he had tried to rein in my folly, I thought

Leto was right. "I actually agree with you, Leto. Jaid is the wisest." My tone switched from playful to serious. "Thank you for being so, Jaid."

Jaid shook his head. "There is nothing to thank me for. We are not out of this yet."

Jaid was right. We were nowhere near being out of our predicament. And I had no idea how to proceed. But since Jaid was a competent guard, maybe he did. "Well, what do you suggest?" I waved my hands in the air. "How do we get out of all this?"

He folded his arms and paced back and forth, bringing his attention to me and Leto. "I do not have a plan, but a plan has presented itself. And I believe we should follow it, with earnest."

Leto quirked a brow. "You speak of the young fae and his plan to kill Malena?"

"I do," he nodded. "She must be stopped."

Leto rubbed his chin and said to me, "You said we would go along with his plan, though I did hear the hesitation in your voice."

"Yes, I hesitated, but only because I did not see any another solution at the time but to join his plan. But you must know I do not know if I can end Malena. I am not like her, nor do I want to be. Even after all that she has done. Yet I agree that she must be stopped."

Jaid continued pacing. "We do not have to decide that now. But since Malena is the heir apparent to Strong Haven, she must go to the Council of Five for the formality of presentation. I am sure Alexander will be with her."

"And probably Draven," Leto tacked on.

"Goshh, nosh Shraven," slurred Manny, his head lolling to the side. "He'shh a shmaniac." Saliva started dripping from his lips. He flopped his hand toward his mouth to wipe it but smacked himself in the eye. "Shwhat the?"

"Do not speak, Manny," I said with a chuckle, dabbing my sleeve against his mouth. "You are coming out of a stupor."

"A shwhat?"

Leto chuckled. "He is actually funny, this one. When he is not irritating."

Leto was right. Manny brought much levity to our dire situation, and I vowed to get him home safely. He did not deserve to be stuck here.

"There they are," Jaid called, shading his eyes while he studied the horizon. Leaf, Ferna, and Parlan were heading back, with a donkey in tow. Jaid brought his attention to us. "We go along with the plan but keep a sharp eye on the Sublander. Understood? There is something about him that does not sit well with me."

"Nor with me," I added.

"I sense the same thing. Something is amiss," Leto chimed in.

Then Manny said, "A sshtuupor?"

We loaded Manny onto the donkey and tied him to the bridle. With everyone turned away, I slipped off my filthy and ragged wedding gown and slipped on a simple sheath of scratchy brown fabric. We all covered our heads with scarves.

We started for the village, and after a short while, we found ourselves traversing the main road. I thought of what it would mean to take on Malena, because it also meant taking on Draven. How could we take them both on?

Julio. That was how. I pictured his face—gorgeous ember eyes, thick brown hair, and full lips. He was probably at Leto's, looking for a shimmer. I prayed to the sun, moon, and stars for him to find one. Not only did I need him, but so did all of Faevenly.

"*Julio*," I thought. "*Please hurry*."

9

JULIO

Driving with Trent to Leto's had me thinking back to when Manny and I brought Celyse there to get help and she collapsed on the doorstep. Then later how Draven blasted the house with his firebombs. So many awful things had happened at Leto's, but also wonderful things. I got to spend time there with Celyse.

"So, you've been to this guy Leto's house?" Trent asked, pulling me away from my memories.

"A few times."

Trent thrummed his fingers on his jeans. "You don't think this witch guy Draven is gonna show up, do you?"

I didn't want to lie, but I also didn't want to add any extra worry to what we were doing. "Honestly, I think if we hurry, in and out, it'll be fine."

Trent nodded. "In and out. Sounds like a plan."

I thought he wanted to ask me something else, but his phone beeped. He brought it out of his back pocket and started texting.

"Is that your mom?"

"Nah, it's a girl I've been dating."

I glanced at him with a raised brow. "What? You never mentioned a girl to me."

He finished with his message and put his phone back. "There hasn't been much chance. Besides, I only started dating her a few months ago. She goes to school with me. I actually met her the day I moved in."

"Wait, the girl you bumped into with your stack of books?"

Trent angled his body toward me. "That's right. You were there helping me move in." He laughed. "I forgot."

"Thanks a lot."

It was a hot August day when I drove to Houston to help Trent move into his dorm. I remembered him bumping into a girl, but I forgot what she looked like. "Well, remind me about her."

"Her name is Dominique, and she's from Michigan. She has long brown hair and these amazing olive-colored eyes. She's super smart and funny, and we just hit it off."

He sounded swept away and I couldn't help but smile. I'd never seen him so into a girl before. "Dude, are you in love?"

"I think so. I mean, maybe." He punched my arm. "Sounds like you are too."

"Oh, I am," I admitted. "And one day I'm going to marry Celyse"—my voice trailed off— "if everything, you know, turns out okay."

Silence fell on us as the mood in the car changed from light to heavy. "It will, *primo*. I have no doubt."

We didn't speak again for a while as I drove along the dark two-lane road to Lake Travis where Leto lived. My thoughts were locked on the dangers we could be facing, but at the same time trying not to think too much about them.

"So," Trent finally said, "I heard you mention something about a blue energy power coming out of you."

He'd heard a lot of what went down when I repeated the story for our *tias* and *tios*. But I hadn't talked to him about my aura. I wondered if the same thing had ever happened to him.

"This might sound really crazy, but you know how I can see ghosts, right?" I asked.

"Yeah."

"Well," I paused. "Turns out I can tap into my aura and use it like a shield or even a weapon."

Trent turned in his seat to face me. "What do you mean?"

Taking my right hand off the wheel, I opened and closed it a few times. "It's hard to explain, but a freakin' powerful blast of blue came out of my hands when we were attacked." Glancing at Trent, I saw his brows stitch and his head tilt. "I guess that hasn't happened to you?"

"Uh . . . no." He looked down at his hands. "But maybe it's inside of me too and I just haven't tapped into it. I mean, all I do is go to class. It's not like my life has been in danger."

We chatted more about powers, and stuff our families could do, laughing and joking as if we were only catching up and our lives weren't in peril. But as we got closer to our destination, the conversation dwindled, the gravity of our situation muting us.

The sky had darkened as we pulled up to Leto's house. But the scorched remains of the small cottage were easy to see amidst the trees and shrubbery.

"Whoa, you weren't kidding," Trent muttered, staring at Draven's destruction with his mouth hung open. "I guess this guy Draven really has a thing for burning stuff."

I parked in front of the house, still taking in the sight. "Your regular psychotic witchy pyromaniac."

Trent reached down for the flashlights on the floorboard and handed one to me. We got out of the car, turned them on, and walked toward the house.

"What are we looking for exactly?" Trent asked.

The beams of light crisscrossed and bounced, bobbing with each step as we neared the house. "A glowy round orb. Kinda like a giant bubble."

Our lights scanned the front of the house, revealing nothing but charred wood, broken glass, and tumbled bricks. The smell of ash and soot invaded my nostrils.

"Let's try the back," I suggested, tramping my way to the side of the house. "I think he may have stashed some orbs away in the woods."

"The woods?"

"Celyse had an orb and I think he brought it back here. I also saw him walk into the woods after his house caught on fire."

"Well, let's see then."

We slipped between the trees, flashing our lights back and forth, when a glimmer in the distance caught my attention. "Over here," I called excitedly.

We dashed to the spot and saw nestled between some bushes a gleaming white plate, a copper mug, bushels of flowers, and shiny stones of purple, white, and pink.

"What the hell?" Trent asked.

"A shrine of some sort? Or an offering?" I guessed, wondering why something like this would be out here. I shifted the plate with my tip of my tennis shoe.

"Someone made an offering to your friend?" he asked.

I shrugged. "I guess so." But then something else occurred to me. "Or maybe it's the other way around. Maybe Leto made an offering to something that's out *here*."

Trent gulped. "Something like what?"

"I have no idea," I said in a hushed voice. "But I'd rather not find out, so let's hurry."

We continued on, weaving our way in and out of the trees and brush, when a tingle struck the back of my neck. I stopped and swung my light around.

"What is it?" Trent followed his light with mine. "Did you hear something?"

"No," I whispered. "But I felt something."

"Uhh, that's not good."

The tingle faded, but its remnants lingered at my hairline. "Let's hurry."

We walked with purpose, scanning the area swiftly,

flinging our flashlights from side to side. Sweat began dotting my forehead and trickling down my chest. I was about to tell Trent we should leave and return in the morning when a shadowy streak darted through the trees.

"Did you see that?" I asked, following the zip with my light, my heart catapulting.

Trent jerked his head in the direction I was staring, then followed my light with his. "What was it?"

A hard wind swept through the trees, rustling the leaves and snapping the branches. One fell from above and whacked the back of my head with a thud.

"What the hell?" I grunted, touching the spot with my fingertips, then flashed the light on my hand to see if there was any blood. Luckily, there wasn't. I already had cuts and scratches on my forehead, face, and neck and didn't need a gash on the back of my head too.

"You all right?" Trent asked.

"I'm fine."

Another branch zoomed by, heading for Trent. He dove forward, face slamming into dirt, the branch missing him by a hair. He spit out a wad of leaves. "Jesus! Should we leave?"

I helped him to his feet, then scanned the night sky, wondering if a gust from bad weather was to blame for the branches. "I say we look for a bit longer. But let's hurry."

We picked up our pace, flashing our beams across the wooded area, when the tingle at the back of my neck returned. This time, a voice echoed all around us.

"Intruuuderrr."

The word stopped us in our tracks. I turned to Trent. "Did you hear that?"

"Yeah," he uttered. "I heard that."

Everything inside of me said to leave, but at the same time, I knew we couldn't. We had to find that shimmer. Celyse, Manny, and the others were counting on us.

A crack sounded. We looked up and spotted a huge branch hurtling our way. We dove, landing face first into dirt and leaves.

Trent rubbed his chin. "Something doesn't want us out here." He scrambled to his feet while looking up at the trees, as if waiting for another round of bombardment.

I pushed myself up too and we huddled under a massive oak, my heart beating out of control. "Maybe Leto set up magic traps, to keep others out."

"You think your friend Leto is doing this?" Trent asked.

The wind died. The trees quieted. The roaring of my heartbeat thudded in my ears. We stayed close to the oak, peering about in silence, when a new sound filled the air—a soft melodic humming.

"Leto is your friend?" a delicate voice said at our ears.

We spun around and aimed our lights at the tree we had been leaning against when the bark vibrated and moved, as if it were alive.

Trent and I stepped back, speechless, and watched

as the movement quickened and a body of moss and leaves stretched out of the trunk. It was a towering, slender creature made of tree bark with sharply pointed facial features and sparkling yellow eyes. She raised her arm and extended her long, pointed, branchy fingers at us.

"Speak," she said.

"Uh." I swallowed with a blink. "Yes. I know Leto. And yes, he's my friend."

She inspected us with curiosity. "What is his given name?"

"Traeliorn Letormis," I said.

"That is he." She smiled, showcasing her wood-nubbed teeth. "I am Genova, dryad and Keeper of these trees. Who are you?"

"I'm Julio Avila, and this is my cousin, Trent Avila."

She bent down and sniffed the top of my head, then did the same to Trent's. "Mere humans." She sniffed again. "But with special gifts." She sniffed us one more time, then brought her face so close to mine, our noses almost touched. She smelled liked leaves and herbs, the scent reminding me of my mom's kitchen and the jars of cuttings and remedies she kept in the cabinets. "You have been to Faevenly?" she asked with wide eyes.

"I have," I said.

She stepped back from us and spun in a circle, the twigs and leaves that formed her long hair lifting with her motion. She brought her face close to mine again.

"It is a glorious place, filled with magic and wonder. Is that where Traeliorn is? I have not seen him in days."

"Yes, he's there, with other fae and my friend Manny."

She stood tall, then glanced in the direction of his house. "Great harm was done to his dwelling. Tell me, is Traeliorn safe?"

I rubbed the back of my neck, wondering how much I should say to her. "Well, I need to go to him and find out. He might be in danger. That's why we're here. We're looking for a shimmer."

"Oh." She backed away from us and placed her hands together in front of her. "I am sad to hear this. I do not wish danger on him."

"Do you know where one is?" Trent asked, stepping forward. "A shimmer? Because we really need one."

She strolled around us in a circle, her movements slow and graceful, her mossy steps padding softly against the grass. "I do indeed know where one is. But Traeliorn gave me strict—"

She stopped mid-sentence and planted in place. She turned her head up to the sky and sniffed the air. "Dear Nature, he is near."

She didn't even have to tell me who she was talking about. "Draven the witch?"

"Yes, the very one," she confirmed, her eyes snapping to me. She tiptoed around us. "Turn off your torches," she whispered.

We shut off our flashlights, then strained our ears

for any evidence of movement. Trent pressed against me and whispered. "Should we run for the car?"

The dryad swung her head toward us. The glimmer from her yellow eyes lit up her face, showcasing the different shades of green in the leaves and moss that made up her skin.

"No running," she hissed. She kept still, letting her warning sink in, then she straightened her body. She extended her arms and beckoned for us to follow her.

Trent and I stayed close, following Genova as quietly as possible, when a tingle connected at my neck. It cascaded through my body with fierce intensity. A second later, my phone blared my mom's ringtone—*Bidi Bidi Bom Bom*.

I dropped my flashlight and dug my hand into my back pocket, turning off the call and silencing my phone. Genova crouched low and brought her face close to mine again, the mossy leaves above her eyes angled into a sharp frown.

She hissed, then righted herself. Trent and I stood as still as possible, holding our breath until the heavy quiet returned. We studied the darkness but saw no signs of movement. A sigh of relief trickled out of me, when the flapping of wings and cawing of birds exploded in all directions.

"He is here!" Genova called out in alarm, breaking into long strides.

Trent and I whipped our heads to face each other, then raced after her, struggling to keep up with her, darting and weaving around trees and brush as best we could in the dark. Finally, she stopped at a mound of dense foliage, like a grassy dune. She placed her hands on the shrubbery. The vines and leaves rustled, then parted like a curtain.

"In, in," she beckoned.

I jumped through and crashed to the ground as a shrill sound pierced the air, followed by a thud and a howl from my cousin.

"Trent!" I shouted, scrambling to get up. A burst of blue light covered the opening, and in another flash, the branches and leaves closed, and darkness enveloped me. "Trent! Genova!"

With my heart beating wildly, I clawed at the spot where the opening had been, but the vines were too thick. I punched and kicked, but nothing was working. I sank to my knees, my body trembling and my thoughts running wild.

"Calm," I repeated. "Stay calm."

I had no idea what was happening outside of my woodsy fae hideout, but I had to believe Trent and Genova were fine and that the blue light I saw was Trent somehow tapping into his abilities. It was better than thinking the alternative.

With the darkness seeming to grow even darker, and my heart thrumming out of control, I drew my phone out of my back pocket, clicked, and pressed, but nothing lit up. It was dead.

"Great," I muttered.

Resisting the urge to chuck it, I stuffed it back in its place, my mind racing with ideas on what I should do, when a speck of light flashed in front of me. The glow held for a minute, revealing a cavernous green space with a dirt floor. It flickered for a few moments, then faded. A few seconds later, another hint of light shone, and not far from that, another. Marveling at the sight, I realized the lights were illuminating in a row, as if showing me a path.

"I'm thinking y'all are some sort of fae fireflies," I said in a hushed tone. "And I'm supposed to follow you."

With more and more of the lightning bugs activated, I followed them across the open space and to a cluster of rocks. Sifting through the rubble, I noticed a latched door underneath, leading to what looked like an underground space.

"Clever Leto," I mumbled.

Lifting the heavy door with a creak, I climbed in and made my way down the packed-dirt steps, a soft light at the bottom growing brighter with my descent. Reaching the floor, I saw rows and rows of glowing orbs of all different shapes and sizes lined up on a wall of shelves.

"Whoa. It's the motherload of shimmers," I uttered.

I approached the display and studied each one closely but couldn't see anything on the other side. They were all too dense, as if filled with clouds.

"I guess I'll have to do this the Avila way," I said to myself.

I raised my hands and held them before the shimmers. I concentrated on Faevenly—the lush greenery, the bright skies, the clean fresh air. Even the memory of the delicious stew I'd had at Leto's cottage came to mind. Lastly, I thought of beautiful Celyse, and closed my eyes.

"Which one?" I asked, moving my hands back and forth in front of the shelves. "Which shimmer?"

It didn't take long for warmth to connect at my palms, followed by a soft pulling sensation. I opened my eyes and saw my hand had almost settled on one of the bigger orbs on the bottom shelf. I cupped it and moved to the center of the room. I grabbed the soft edges that felt like an energy-filled sheathing and tugged. When the shimmer stretched long enough and wide enough for me to fit through, I took a giant gulp.

"All right," I said, "I'm coming."

10

MALENA

My eyes were wide as I lay on my side, gazing at the narrow opening between the panels of my silk curtains. The dark gap signaled night, but my mind resisted slumber, choosing instead to race with worry about going before the Council of Five. Alexander had said some of the provinces would not be supporting me as successor to the High Throne. He had even gone to Cuesta with his father to garner support for me, and for himself as future High King, but I had not heard from him in two days. I prayed to the sun, moon and stars he had found success.

Turning to my back, I let out a sigh. At daybreak, I would prepare for my journey to Strong Haven West, where the Council of Five convened twice a year—sometimes more often if circumstances warranted. Even though it was under Strong rule, no sitting Strong family had ever occupied the province. Every Strong had ruled from the east and only visited the west for respite and holiday excursions. It was also the region that encompassed Quietus Valley, where the wolfbeasts roamed.

I was eager to get to the west so I could set the

foolish lords of the provinces in their places. It was the Strongs who had brought about a time of peace in Faevenly after the Great Shimmer War and established the council. Without my family, they would be nothing. And I was going to do everything in my power to remind them of that.

With my mind adrift, I detected a hazy gray between my curtains, and sighed even deeper. Rest would not be coming for me after all. It was just as well. The journey to Strong Haven West would take at least three days. I could slumber on the way, if needed, in the carriage. There would also be an overnight stop in High Meadow and then again in Cuesta.

The gray between my curtains lightened to a soft white, and the day was officially upon me. I turned my thoughts to Draven. I had planned to call on him upon leaving the palace grounds to request his presence at the Council of Five meeting. I would need his help with persuasion and influence. With Alexander and House Kane on one side of me, and Draven on the other, none would challenge me.

The door to my bedchamber creaked open. Staying still, I watched Maid Gidna ease into my bedchamber with a tray of fresh water. Her feet padded against the marble floors as she crossed the room. She placed her tray on my side table with a clink, then proceeded to open my curtains.

"High Queen, it is time to start the day," she said in a near whisper.

I flung off my covers and rubbed my eyes. She was

right. I needed to get myself in motion. “Maid Gidna, please prepare a washing station in my dressing chamber.”

She bowed low. “Of course.”

Forcing myself to act every bit the queen, I held my head high, donned my silk robe, and made my way to my dressing chamber. Several young maids were bustling about, preparing my dresses and packing my trunks. They curtsied low when I walked in.

“High Queen,” the tallest one said. “We have prepared your dresses. May we present them for your approval?”

“Yes, you may,” I said, taking a seat on the chaise in the middle of the room.

She held up a dark blue, long-sleeved dress with a square neckline and an ankle-length hem. “We thought this would be the most comfortable travel attire for your first day. Not too ornate or heavy, and made of the softest silk. Does this meet with your approval?”

She held it out for me, and I ran my fingers along the smooth fabric. The selection reminded me of a dress Mother wore once when we traveled to Summit Range for the butterfly festival. I loved it so much, I asked for one just like it to be made for me because I wanted to be just like her. Now, I would be donning a similar dress, no longer pretending to be like Mother, but stepping into her role. I thought she would approve.

“The dress is perfect.”

Another maid interrupted the presentation. “High Queen, your bath is ready.”

With the bath waiting for me on the far end of the dressing chamber, the maids began setting the dresses aside. I stopped them with an order. “I would like to see my dress for my appearance before the Council of Five before I wash.”

The tall maid gulped, then nodded. “Yes, High Queen.”

With the help of the other maids, she brought out a sleeveless purple dress with a plunging neckline and a sheath skirt. It was paired with a dramatic purple cape of the same fabric adorned with dazzling crystals.

“I hope this meets your request for classic and regal, High Queen,” she said.

The dress exceeded my expectations, and I envisioned every member of the council admiring me with jealousy and longing. “It is magnificent.”

With a smile, the young maid set the dress back in its place. “May I escort you to your bath now?”

“You may.”

She followed me to the oversized tub and helped me get in. The warm water soothed my tired muscles, and the aroma from the roses and lavender floating on top calmed my senses. But I had no time to dawdle; there was much to do before my departure.

After a short soak, I slipped on a robe and took a seat so Maid Gidna could work on my hair. She brushed my long silver locks, then braided two thin pieces in the front and tied them together at the back.

With my hair finished, the smallest maid got to work on my face. She applied an ivory cream all over, then dusted my cheeks with a pearlescent pink powder. She finished with soft beiges and blues on my eyelids.

She held a mirror before me. "Is it to your liking?"

Maid Gidna and the other maids were still learning my tastes. And even though none of them had the same skill set as Maid Rell, I knew they would get better with time. "It is adequate. Thank you."

She smiled. "I am so glad. Now to put on your dress and apply the oils."

She stood on a stool and helped slip the dress over my head. It fell perfectly into place, hugging my statuesque figure in all the right places. She fastened the buttons in the back, then retrieved a silver tray of oils. I picked up the vials, my thoughts whisking me to Celyse and how I had always helped her pick her scent, but I quickly shut them down.

She was a vile human, a product of my father's indiscretion. She was nothing to me, and soon would be dead. I needed to not forget that.

"High Queen, are the selections not to your liking?"

My attention snapped to the young maid assessing me with concern and a touch of fear as my hand hovered over the vials. I lifted one up. "I am sure they are fine."

Her face relaxed and I opened the vial. I held it to my nose, drawing in the sweet aroma of roses, lilies, and wisteria. I did not even have to smell the other options; this combination was perfect.

"This is the one," I announced, opening it and dabbing the oil on my wrists, behind my ears, and at the back of my neck. When I was finished, I gave her the vial. "Please pack this in my things."

"Yes, High Queen."

Fully dressed and with my things packed, I was ready for breakfast. I exited my dressing chamber, nodded to Windon, and made my way down the corridor to the staircase. Once downstairs, I weaved my way through the garden to a table spread with jams, fruits, nuts, and juices.

With the meal servants at the ready, I paused for a few long seconds, thinking of all the times I had sat here with my once perfect family. What a fool I had been.

One of the meal servants pulled my seat out and waited for me to move. She cleared her throat. "Does this setting meet your approval?"

Snapping back to what was expected of me, I sat down, "It does."

The meal servants began bustling about me. "High Queen, would you like apple cranberry juice this morning? Or berry orange?"

I unfolded my napkin and placed it on my lap. "Berry orange."

The meal servant filled my glass, then stepped back. Telling myself I was fine being alone, I served myself maple-dipped strawberries, sliced kiwi, and rosemary muffins. I took slow and steady bites, savoring the sweetness of the food. After eating only a bit, I found myself full and pushed my chair away from the table. As soon as I draped my napkin over my plate and stepped away, the meal servants swooped in to clean. I noticed there were only two serving me instead of the usual four. I was about to ask where the others were when Maid Gidna approached.

"High Queen," she said. "Your things have been stored on the carriages, and everything is ready for your departure."

"Thank you," I nodded.

My spirits elevated some at the idea of travel. A reprieve from the gloom that had been cast on Strong Haven East would do me well. That, and I loved a journey—the change in scenery, the adventure of being on the open road, not to mention the pomp and circumstance of the Strong entourage.

As the highest rulers over all of Faevenly, the Strongs traveled in dramatic fashion, with four outfitted royal coaches. The first coach had a guard detail, the second coach carried the royal family, the third held the royal servants, and the fourth contained another guard detail.

Boarded and ready to depart, I was overcome with a new feeling—power. I could hardly wait for the Council of Five to see me. And if any one of them defied me, they would be ended.

11
JULIO

My body hurtled into a free fall, then slammed into a grassy surface. I sputtered out dirt and a few blades of grass before lifting myself up on my elbows and looking around. Fireflies danced all around me. They flickered on and off, illuminating the lush greenery and brilliant flowers. Overhead, the clear and crisp night sparkled with hundreds of stars, and the cleanest air filtered into my lungs.

I was most definitely in Faevenly.

I scrambled to my feet, then studied the floating shimmer before me. Like I'd seen Celyse do, I placed my fingertips on the edges and slowly gathered it together until it was the size of a baseball. Not exactly knowing what to do with it, I spotted a cluster of rose bushes. I cupped the electric bubble, walked it over there, and placed it on the ground in the middle of the flowers, scooping a handful of leaves and covering it from sight.

With that done, I studied the landscape, hoping to see something familiar so I could remember this location for later. Instead, I spotted a trail of smoke. It was either coming from a chimney or a camp. And it wasn't too far off.

"Please," I mumbled, patting my shirt where my cross hung. "Not a bad guy."

Taking off toward the source, I trudged through the meadow. As I walked, the landscape started morphing from lush to sparse. Even the smells changed from dirt and grass to dirt and . . . lake water? A few more steps, and I heard the rippling flow of a steam. I stopped and studied the area again, suddenly realizing where I was.

"The Green Falls," I said with a smile. Now I knew how Leto kept some of the Green Falls liquid in his house. He had his own doorway to the place.

As I got closer to the smoke, my steps grew slower and more cautious. What if the smoke was leading me to Draven? Wouldn't that suck?

Advancing forward, I spied a campfire between some brush. I crouched down to the ground to scope it out. Rocks circled the fire, and nearby lay a small pack. Just beyond grazed a magnificent black horse.

"Do not move," a deep voice warned.

I froze. "Okay."

"Turn around."

I straightened, then shuffled my feet around and met the hulky guy Celyse was faking her marriage with —Rook. He held a dagger at the ready, his face in a snarl.

"You," he said, keeping his defensive posture. "The human witch."

"Um, yeah. Me. My name is Julio Avila."

He shoved the dagger in my face. "Declare your intent, Julio Avila, human witch."

"I'm here to save Celyse and my friend Manny, and Jaid, Leto, Ferna, and Parlan." Giving him the once over, thinking he looked like crap, I thought he needed saving too. "And anyone else who needs help."

He lowered his weapon. "I am Rook Cailean."

He had looked strong and vibrant at the wedding, but shrouded in darkness with only the stars overhead and the nearby campfire for light, he resembled someone from a zombie movie. His skin was as white as death, and blood was splattered all over his gold shirt.

"I thought you were"—I gulped— "dead."

He moved back to the fire, his footsteps slow and laborious. "I was stabbed and died and was reborn. I escaped the palace and came here to be healed."

He sat by the fire and motioned for me to take a seat across from him.

"You were reborn?" I asked.

He poked the fire with a stick, sending a rush of crackling flames and pops into the air. "Yes. I died, but I did not stay dead. I have been ingesting small amounts of water from the Green Falls since I was a mere boy to help me maintain fae-like longevity and strength. It must have given me the added bonus of coming back from the dead."

"Fae-like?" I tilted my head.

"Yes, fae-like. I am a human, like you."

"Whoa," I whispered, thinking I'd heard it all. "You?" I asked, pointing at him. "Are a human?"

He poked the fire again. "I am."

My head spun, my mind formulating a ton of follow-up questions, but Rook didn't want to talk. "Now that you are here, please watch the fire so I may sleep."

He lay on his side, moved his pack under his head, and closed his eyes.

I stayed in my spot for a while, not exactly knowing what to do, before getting up and retrieving Rook's fire poker. I started stoking the flames. If Rook was out here alone, looking like death warmed over, then the area was most definitely safe. Especially since Rook didn't give any warnings otherwise. Plus, I remembered how the Green Falls was kind of a hidden place.

Studying the flames, my mind went to Trent, wondering if he was okay. And then it drifted to Celyse, Manny, and the others imprisoned in the Sublands. As soon as Rook was awake, I'd ask him to help me free them.

With my nerves still riled up, I decided I needed to do something, like get wood. I worked my way around our camp, picking up twigs and branches. Soon, I had an armful of kindling. I brought my finds back and set them near the fire but thought I could use a few bigger pieces. Venturing a little farther out, I treaded through the grassy flatland and came upon a good-sized log. I scooped it up with both arms, then turned and saw my mom. The log slipped out of my arms, but I snatched it back up before it hit my toes.

"Mom!"

"*Mijo!*" she said with surprised relief.

A haze filtered through her skin, reminding me of the ghosts I could see. But of course, I knew she wasn't. I would have felt something. "Are you okay?"

"I am. I'm sending my spirit to you from the cabin. I wanted to make sure you were okay, and let you know that Trent made it back."

A sigh of relief escaped my lips. "Oh, thank goodness. I was so worried."

She nodded. "I know. That's why I had to come to you." She moved in closer. "Now that I have, I must go. I don't want that evil man locking in on you or me. Okay?"

"Okay."

"One more thing. You find Manny and Celyse, and then you send your spirit to me and let me know. I will find a way to help you all get back," she said.

"I will."

"I love you, *mijo*."

"Love you, Mom."

She disappeared in a flash, leaving me relieved that Trent had made it and glad she was working on her end to get me and the others out of here. All I needed to do was get to them.

I went back to the fire and plunked the log on the middle of the small flames, then placed a few sticks on all sides, forming a small pyre. The blaze crackled and whooshed as the flames expanded and lengthened, the musky scent of smoke and leaves twirling around me.

My gazed roamed the quiet landscape for a while before settling on Rook and his blood-stained clothes. Thinking of my own injuries, I brought my fingertips to my face, prodding at the cuts along my forehead, cheeks, and neck. Even my lip felt bruised and puffy from when I smashed it on the sidewalk back in Baltimore and again on the ground here. I pondered the falls. The waters had saved Celyse and now Rook. Surely the liquid could heal my cuts.

I eased myself away from the fire and headed toward the sound of the cascading waters that grew louder with each step. I soon came upon a trodden path through the brush and found myself quickly at the water's edge. In the dark, the water glowed, and I watched the tumbling liquid empty into a pool of green as memories of when I was last here rushed to my mind. I had carried Celyse into the water to be healed, and then kissed her and survived, even though a fae kiss was deadly to humans.

If she were here with me now. I'd kiss her again.

Reining in my desires, I bent over and cupped my hands together. I dunked them under the water, brought out a scoopful, and splashed my face. The cool liquid felt cleansing and refreshing against my aching skin, almost like a liquid salve. Stripping off my shirt, I tossed it to the side and scooped more handfuls and doused my face and neck. I even ran a few handfuls through my hair.

That should do it.

Stepping away from the water, I was headed back toward Rook when I spotted a boulder not too far away. Large and round, about the size of a small car, it looked like the perfect spot to keep an eye on Rook but also enjoy the sounds of the Green Falls.

I climbed on top, set my shirt aside to dry off, then perched myself as if I were a guardian or protector. The roaring of the Green Falls eased me a little, as did the crackling of the fire, and soon my thoughts were consumed with Celyse. I could almost smell her and feel her soft velvety lips against mine. Suddenly, I thought of something. If my mom could project my spirit to her, maybe I could do that on my own. Maybe I didn't need help.

"Okay," I mumbled to myself. "Let's try this."

I crossed my legs and drew in deep, long breaths, slowing my heart as I let go of the tension in my body. When a sense of peace filled me, I concentrated on Celyse. I pictured her long silver hair with the streak of black, her soft and smooth skin, her luscious lips. Her image formed perfectly in my mind with such precision and clarity, I was standing behind her.

"Celyse."

She spun around, her eyes wide as a smile spread across her beautiful face. "Julio!"

We instinctively reached for each other, but our arms passed through our bodies. A small laugh escaped her lips as she backed up, her gaze landing on my chest. A hint of pink spread across her cheeks and her lips parted some before she brought her eyes up to mine.

She cleared her voice and brushed the hair from her face. "Julio."

If we were together, nothing would have stopped me from kissing her. But we weren't together. And our circumstances could not have been more dire.

"Celyse, I am so glad to see you."

"Me too." She bridged the gap between us.

A mere inch apart, I found it hard to concentrate, but forced myself to. "I'm here, in Faevenly."

Her eyes sparkled with surprise. "In Faevenly? Where?"

"The Green Falls, of all places. And guess who's with me?"

Her brows stitched together. "Who?"

"Rook."

She gasped and brought her hands to her mouth. She held them there for a few seconds before lowering them. "But he was killed at Strong Haven Palace. Maid Rell said so herself."

"He was, but he didn't stay dead. He's been drinking water from the Green Falls since he was a boy, and it somehow brought him back to life. He came here to get more. Now he's asleep."

"Incredible," she muttered.

I noticed she had changed out of her wedding dress and into a plain brown one. She also looked like she'd had a shower. Her face was clean, and her hair sparkled with a shiny glow. Looking around, I saw she wasn't in a cell anymore, but in a small room with a cot and a chair.

"Where are you?" I asked.

"We have escaped. We rented a room at an inn near the Sublands. We are all together and well and with a young fae named Leaf, who is helping us. We have decided to confront Malena. We travel in the morning to Strong Haven West, where the Council of Five is scheduled to meet in two days."

"Confront her how?"

A rumble shook the ground beneath my feet. In a rush, my senses were pulled away from Celyse and brought back to the boulder where thunder crackled overhead and a furious wind whipped around me. I scrambled down from my perch, slipping on my shirt, and rushed over to Rook. He was on his feet, hands fisted, ready for hand-to-hand combat.

"What is happening?" he roared.

Every time I had used my power to see Celyse, I had been torn away. I had to believe it was Draven somehow tracking me. It was as if my energy was a beacon, and he was my predator.

"It's Draven!" I hollered.

"Draven the witch?" He spun around, searching. "Where? How?"

The earth continued shaking, my mind scrambling with what to do, when suddenly everything stopped. I sank to my knees, sighing with relief.

"He must have locked in on me when I used my gifts. Or he almost locked in on me." I peered up at the sky, as if I'd see some sort of evidence of Draven's tracking methods, but only saw bright stars.

"You used your gifts?" he asked incredulously.

"Yes," I answered, bringing my attention back on Rook. "I visited Celyse in spirit form."

He relaxed his stance and turned a sharp eye on me. "Are you sure you are only a human?"

I rubbed the back of my neck, thinking of my family and the stuff we could do. "I'm sure."

"But you visited her in spirit form?" he asked.

"I did. It's a long story how I can do that, but it happened. You just have to trust me, okay?"

Rook considered me and gave me a slow nod. "Where is she? What is happening with her?"

"She's with my friend Manny and Jaid, Leto, Ferna, Parlan, and a fae named Leaf. They are near the Sublands but heading to Strong Haven West in the morning. They plan to confront Malena."

Rook rubbed his face. "Good. It is my intent to do the same. And I know Leaf. He is one of my trusted allies. We will rendezvous with them. Now, please, no more spirit visits or any other witchy escapades. If I am to heal properly, I need rest."

Just like that, he was back on the ground. Two blinks later, snoring filled the air. But there was no way I could fall asleep quickly. Draven was on to me. And with him out there, none of us were safe.

12
CELYSE

I exploded out of my quarters and into the common area of our small room. "We have to go!"

Jaid and Leto jumped to their feet, daggers drawn. Manny was recovering from his stupor, asleep on a cot, but jerked his head up with a start. Ferna, Parlan, and Leaf started grabbing our packs.

"What is it?" Jaid asked, running into the room I had come from.

"Draven may be on to us," I warned, grabbing his arm and pulling him out.

Manny's tan face turned white. "D-D-Draven?"

"Everyone out!" Jaid hollered.

Scrambling with our things, we dashed out of our room and down the narrow hallway, then busted out the front door. We had planned for a quick departure anyway, and earlier in the day had secured horses, weapons, clothes, and food, but now was as good a time as any to take off.

When we were loaded up and on our horses, Leto kicked the sides of his beast and clicked his tongue. "Ride!"

We headed west, crouched low as we raced into the

darkness. When the village was far behind us, we eased up until we eventually stopped.

"What in the hell?" Manny asked, sliding off his horse and emptying the contents of his stomach several times over. He stayed hunched over for a while with his hands on knees. "Y'all can't do that crap to me!"

Catching my breath, I apologized. "I am sorry, Manny. But it was necessary. Julio visited me again. He is here in Faevenly now, at the Green Falls, and with Rook. I told him we were headed for Strong Haven West. Before we could talk further, a force pulled him away from me. I believe it was Draven."

Manny wiped his mouth with his sleeve. "A force pulled him away?" He blinked. "And Rook is alive?"

"Yes," I said. "A force pulled him away, but I am confident he is fine."

Leaf trotted his horse around to face me, his eyes bright with hope. "Rook is not dead?"

"He is not. He is alive thanks to his use of water from the Green Falls," I explained.

"Incredible," Jaid murmured.

"He is full of surprises, that one," Leto agreed.

"Julio said they are heading to the Council of Five to confront Malena," I said.

Our horses circled around, still fired up from the charge. "Well, let's keep going!" Leaf prodded excitedly. "The sooner we can get to Strong Haven West, the better."

After two days of hard travel, which included a

tedious journey over the Great Peaks, we finally crossed into Strong Haven West. Apprehension and unease twisted my gut. I was not sure if I was ready to see Malena or the rest of the council. My father had been executed for his misdeeds with the shimmers, misdeeds I too had committed. What would they do when they saw me?

"We will camp here for the night," Jaid announced, slowing his horse at a grassy clearing surrounded by trees and brush.

Everyone dismounted. Leto and Jaid walked the perimeter; Manny and Leaf searched for stones to fashion a campfire border; and Ferna, Parlan, and I gathered wood. With everything set up, and nightfall upon us, we settled around the fire and passed around a loaf of bread.

Jaid took a piece, then started the conversation. "We need a strategy. We will not be well received showing our faces before Malena after having been banished. She will surely have Draven with her. And Alexander."

"We're gonna die there, aren't we," Manny muttered, taking the loaf from Jaid and tearing of a large chunk and shoving it into his mouth.

"We are not going to die there," Leto said. "Violence is not allowed at the meetings of the Council of Five. It is a neutral space."

"Really?" Manny wiped his forehead and blew out. "That's good to know. But what exactly is the Council of Five?"

I angled my body toward Manny. "The Council of Five is made up of the stewards of each of the five provinces—Strong Haven, Sand Bluff, High Meadow, Cuesta, and Summit Range. While Strong Haven rules over all of Faevenly, each province has its own family that acts as overseers."

"But each province answers to Strong Haven, so it is not exactly independent governing," Leaf added in a tone laced with antagonism. He passed the bread, then picked up a stick and jabbed at the fire. "The provinces may as well be prisoners to the Strongs."

Leaf had every right to be angry. Now that I knew the atrocities my father and the High Queen had been committing against humans, and even the Sublands, I wondered what else they were doing. I was sure there were other malfeasances attributable to House Strong.

"So . . ." Manny said, slightly raising an eyebrow at Leaf before turning his attention to me. "What is going to happen tomorrow? What's the big meeting for?"

"It is for the formal presentation of Malena as the successor of Strong Haven," Leto answered.

"And we have to stop her at all costs," Leaf asserted.

"Okayyy, so how are we going to stop her without violence?" Manny asked.

I stared into the flames, thinking Manny's question a good one. "Since we cannot fight, we have to use our words. Urge the provinces to not recognize Malena as heir and instead find a new Faevenly ruler amongst the other houses."

"What about you?" Manny asked.

I balked. "Me? No, no, no. I am half human and would never be approved. The new ruler must be a full-blooded fae. Not that I even want that role."

"I knew it," Leaf hissed. "You do not even care for this land."

Jumping to my feet, I retorted, "I most certainly do!"

Jaid raised himself to his feet and stood beside me. "Ease up, Leaf, or you will find yourself on the wrong end of my dagger. Your quarrel is not with Celyse. Or anyone here for that matter."

Leaf narrowed his eyes at Jaid, then marched off. I sat back down, and so did Jaid.

"Young and foolish," Ferna said with a shake of her head, passing the bread to Parlan.

"Foolish fae end up dead fae," Jaid warned.

Leto threw Jaid a sidelong glance, then picked up our conversation. "Asking the other provinces to move against House Strong with House Kane behind her will not be an easy task."

"The argument will have to be compelling," Jaid said.

"By now they all know of my father's crimes of tampering with shimmers," I said. "But I wonder if they know of the extent. Maybe if they knew, they would disavow Malena and anyone standing with her."

"That might work," Jaid said. "But what of Strong Haven? Maybe Leaf has a point, and you should stay and rule. The fact that you are not a full-blooded fae be damned."

My heart sank. Rule Faevenly? And forget the human realm? I wanted to do right by Faevenly, but I also wanted to do right by me. I did not think ruling would accomplish either of those things.

"Never mind that for now," Leto interjected, saving me from that conversation. "Let us figure out how to get the other provinces to disavow Malena."

"Easy," Manny offered. "It's like my favorite show, *Survivor*. You make an alliance. Get one of the other houses to stand with us."

Jaid rose to his feet and walked around the fire. "That is not a bad idea. With High Meadow supporting Malena, and Sand Bluff probably supporting her too since the undead High Queen is from there, that leaves Summit Range and Cuesta."

I had no idea what Manny meant by saying he had a favorite show called *Survivor*, but I understood the rest. An ally would change everything. "Cuesta," I said without hesitation. "Jorn Lind attacked me, which means their house has no loyalty to the Strongs."

"But I killed their son," Jaid said.

"That is true. But you were serving House Strong, and now no longer do. You are a renegade like the rest of us."

A stretch of silence set in while everyone considered the conversation. Manny broke the quiet. "So, we go to this big meeting and try to convince another house to join us in opposing Malena as the new High Queen."

"That is correct," I said.

"Sounds easy enough," Manny shrugged. Then he added, "Is there any bread left?"

I wanted it to be easy, but nothing ever was. The evening went on with much chatter about how to sneak onto the grounds of Strong Haven West, how to manage a private audience with Lord and Lady Lind from Cuesta, how to meet up with Julio and Rook, and how to not get killed.

After much debate, which included Leaf who had returned with his anger somewhat in check, the overriding decision was to figure everything out when we arrived at the palace.

Or, as Manny said, wing it.

THE STRONG HAVEN WEST MANOR WAS SMALLER THAN the Strong Haven East Palace, by a great measure. Built in a simple square shape, the junior palace of tan and gray stone had only two floors with five rooms on the first floor and six on the second. The kitchen, dining room, receiving room, study and library were on the first floor. The bedchambers were all on the second. The grounds were filled with shrubs and flowers with concrete benches, and a large pond sprawled in the back. Lady Wren and her mate, Lord Delfin, served as custodians, and a small staff was at their disposal.

Studying the manor house from a distance at an elevated vantage point, I counted four carriages and several footmen and valets. The Strong carriages had not yet arrived.

"What now?" Ferna asked.

While Jaid stroked his chin, an idea came to me. I faced the group. "This is going to sound mad, but with Malena not there yet, what if we simply march in?"

"Whoa," Manny said. "Hold up. March in like, 'Hey, what's up? How's everyone doing?' Or march in like, 'We're here to kill you!'"

"The first one," I said.

Jaid and Leto glanced at each other before bringing their attention to me. "I actually think that might work," Leto said.

"What about Alexander and his family?" Parlan asked.

"What about them?" Leaf said with fury. "They are no better than anyone else."

Jaid lowered his hand from his chin. "I say we do as Celyse suggests. We march in. But we must act fast before Malena arrives."

With daggers at our waists, swords at our sides, and bows and arrows on our backs—except for Manny, who only had a dagger—we mounted our rides and broke into a gallop to the manor house. We slowed when we approached and dismounted where the carriages were stationed. The valets frowned at our arrival, then gaped when they recognized me.

Ignoring them, and pretending I was wearing a gown befitting of my status instead of commoner garb,

I raised my head high and strode with confidence to the oversized double wood carved door.

The doorman swung the door open, his jaw dropping. "Princess Celyse, uh, um, I mean, uh . . ."

I nodded and breezed past the stout dwarf with Jaid and Leto flanking me and the others behind. I crossed the foyer and marched to the receiving room just beyond. Stopping at the entrance, I studied the room.

The white marble floors with gold flecks gleamed from fresh polish. The pearlescent walls sparkled, and rich silver drapes framed the windows that lined the back walls, showcasing the sprawling pond covered in lily pads. Oversized plush silver chairs were set up in a circular pattern. The lords and ladies from the other provinces, in their royal attire, rose to their feet when they spotted me. Most of them were at my fake wedding.

"Seize her!" Alexander shouted, brandishing his sword with a metallic zing and rushing my way.

Strapped with my own sword, I whipped it out. Leaf whipped out his too. Jaid and Leto pulled out their bows and arrows, aiming at Alexander and his father.

Everyone froze.

"No one is seizing me," I declared.

Jaid and Leto stayed close to me as Ferna, Parlan, and Leaf slowly fanned out, their weapons at the ready. I had no idea where Manny was.

"There will be no blood shed here!" Lady Wren

called out from the front of the room, worming her way through the guests and holding her arms out. She wore a long red dress with her silver hair piled up on her head. "It is forbidden!"

The lords and ladies parted, as if leaving the quarrel to me and my troop and Alexander, his father, and the few guards standing behind them. His mother was absent.

I kept my sword pointed at Alexander and his smug face. "I have no intention of shedding blood, but I demand to be heard!"

Leaf sidled in front of me, his blue eyes bearing down on Alexander and his father, his sword raised. "She may not have that purpose. But I have every intention of shedding blood. Especially Kane blood."

Alexander narrowed his eyes. "You," he said to Leaf. "The imprisoned Sublander, thrown into the cages with these banished renegades. If blood is shed, it will be yours first, the others after."

I had no idea what Leaf was up to but did not let it show. Leaf had made a move, and we needed to see it through.

I kept my sword pointed and met eyes with everyone in the room. "I come before you today to see who here will stand against Malena and declare the rule of House Strong as forfeited." Murmuring filled the room. I took that as a positive sign and kept on. "Atrocities have been committed by the Strongs, and they have gravely misused the shimmers against the human realm. A house that cares for this realm and all others should rule instead. Who here is with me?"

Before any could respond, Leaf moved in toward the elder Kane. "You know all about atrocities, Lord Kane," he snarled. "Is that not right?"

Alexander shot his father a questioning look, but before anyone could utter another word, the elder Kane growled, "Enough of this, Leaf!"

Leaf? The elder Lord Kane knew the young imprisoned Sublander?

Leaf advanced by another step. "Enough of me exposing you for the fraud you are? Or enough of Alexander playing a role that does not belong to him? Or maybe enough of the two of you being allowed to breathe air?"

"What is the meaning of this?" demanded Malena, entering the room.

Jaid and I swung around our weapons to meet her, while Leaf, Leto, Ferna, and Parlan kept theirs on Alexander and his father.

"You," Malena hissed, snarling at me, dressed in her usual regal attire.

"Yes, me," I said with a raise of my brow. "Surprise."

Her hands curled into fists at her sides and she yelled, "Kill them!"

13

JULIO

"There they are," I whispered from a bush where Rook and I were hiding. We'd been on the grounds of Strong Haven West for a while now, watching the carriages from the other provinces approach. We scurried from shrub to shrub until we were a stone's throw from where the last carriage was parked.

We were calculating our next move when Celyse and the others charged in on their horses, dismounted, and strode to the front door before we could reach them. Luckily, Manny's shoe caught on his stirrup. With all eyes on the door where Celyse and the others had entered, I swooped out as Manny untangled himself. I slammed one hand over his mouth, and pulled him into the bushes.

"It's me," I hissed at his ear. "Don't yell."

He turned and faced me with wide eyes, and I slowly peeled my fingers off his face. He grabbed my shoulders and hugged me. "Julio! I didn't think I'd ever see you again!"

Rook hushed us. "Look," he said, pointing at the structure.

From our hiding spot, we saw a lone carriage pull up. Malena stepped out, looking smug and confident but also irritated. Four maids emerged after her.

"I cannot believe I am late!" she shrilled at them.

The maids attempted to soothe her while two adjusted a long sparkly cape she wore over an elaborate purple dress, and another two brushed her hair and fixed her makeup.

After quick primping, Malena swatted them away. "Inform the drivers of the other carriages I will have words with them after the meeting. How the wheels shattered like that is beyond me. Someone will pay, and pay dearly!" She started off then hollered over her should, "Alert me when Draven arrives!"

When she disappeared into the house, Rook stood and unsheathed his dagger. "No guards and no witch. Luck is on our side today."

"What are we doing?" Manny asked.

"We are going after Malena and taking her out," Rook growled.

With a swallow, I brandished the dagger Rook had given me. "And saving Celyse."

Manny took out a dagger from a holster at his waist. "And making sure I don't get killed in the process."

"We'll be fine," I assured him in the most confidant tone I could muster.

The three of us hurried for the door while royally dressed leaders started filtering out of the manor house and rushing to their carriages.

Something must've happened.

We squeezed by them and busted in to see utter mayhem had erupted. Arrows whizzed. Swords clanged. Malena crouched low to the ground, hiding, and she wasn't far from me. I shot Manny and Rook a look, then charged at her.

"The High Queen!" someone yelled. "Protect her!"

An arrow zoomed by me, nicking my ear as I lunged, collapsing onto Malena with all my weight. I wrapped my arm around her neck and held her in a chokehold. I scrambled to my feet and dragged her up with me.

Rook flanked me on one side and Manny on the other. Celyse spun in the middle of the room, whipping her sword with ease, slicing the attackers charging her. In that moment, she looked more beautiful than ever.

"Call them off!" I ordered Malena, jerking her neck. "Now!"

She choked out with a grunt, "Stop!"

The clanging subsided. Weapons lowered. Celyse turned and spotted me, her eyes filled with relief and affection. She rushed over to me, and the others followed. They formed a protective circle around me and Malena.

A fae guy with long dark hair and blue eyes kept his sword raised. He was standing with an older fae man that looked like his dad. I was sure I had seen them at the wedding, fighting against us.

"Give the High Queen to me," the younger one said. "And I will let all of you live."

"You are in no position to make demands, Alexander," Celyse declared. "We have Malena, which means we have the upper hand."

"But I am in a position to make demands," a clear voice rang out from behind me.

Twisting around, I saw Draven entering the room, his black cloak swaying, his hood shrouding his face. Celyse eased her sword around and held the tip at Malena's temple.

"Not one step closer, Draven," Celyse threatened.

"Or what?" he asked, taking two more steps before he stopped. He lowered his hood, glaring at Celyse with his diamond-like eyes. "You will kill your half-sister?"

Malena's throat bobbed against my arm as she gulped. "Kill them, Draven!" She cried. "Now!"

I tightened my arm around her neck. "Harm us and she's dead."

Draven flashed us a sinister smirk. "Such a tempting offer from the human witch. But alas, the High Queen is under my protection. As is her mate and his house."

Draven held out his arm and said, "Come now, Alexander." He waved the fae over. "You and yours are with me."

"Let them pass," Jaid instructed, his eyes narrowed and his stance wide as Alexander sheathed his sword, and together with the older fae and a few guards, edged their way over to Draven. When they moved behind him, Draven's lips curled up in a sinister smile.

"Watch him," Leto hissed.

"Watch me do this?" Draven flicked his cape, spinning into a blur, zipping through the room so fast my eyes darted all over until he ended up back where he was . . . with Manny in his grasp.

"No!" I yelled.

"What just happened?" Manny uttered, appearing dizzy and unsteady until he realized he was in Draven's clutches. His eyes widened. He opened his mouth to speak, but nothing came out. He was too terrified, and so was I.

"Now," Draven said with a click of his tongue. "Here is what is going to happen. Listen close. You will release the High Queen, and when you do, I will release this human and we will leave. I will not harm any of you. You have my word."

Celyse kept her sword on Malena. "You cannot be trusted, Draven."

"I assure you," he sneered. "You can trust me on this."

"Deceiver!" blurted a young fae with dark hair and blue eyes who was standing with us. I thought for sure it was the newcomer Celyse said was helping them. A fae named Leaf. Rook said he was an ally. "You trick us with your words! We will make the switch and you will find a way to kill us!"

Draven flicked his wrist. Leaf's sword wrenched out of his hand, spun midair, and pointed at his mouth. Leaf froze but kept his stare glued on Draven.

"Now, human witch," Draven said to me, ignoring everyone else. "Do you agree to the trade?"

I had been working for days to get to Faevenly so I could get Manny back home, and now he was in the clutches of the deadly witch. I glanced at Celyse, my gut twisting so tight I could hardly breathe.

"We have to," I whispered.

Her eyes held mine for a few seconds before she nodded. "I know."

"Go ahead, Julio," Leto encouraged.

"Yeah," Manny squeaked out in a high-pitched voice. "Do the deal."

Looking at Manny, all I could do was think about his dad. I promised him I would bring Manny home, and I was going to fulfill that promise.

Hating what I was about to do, I asked Draven, "I have your word that when I release Malena you will release Manny and all of you will leave without harming any of us?"

Draven nodded nice and slow. "You have my word. And as a showing of my good intentions, I will release first."

He loosened his grip on Manny's neck, then lowered his arms. Manny brought his hands to his throat and drew in a deep breath before slowly walking over to me. When he was safely by my side, Celyse lowered her sword and I released my grip on Malena. She lifted the skirt of her dress and scurried across the room and into Alexander's arms.

Draven smiled. "See? That was not so bad."

The witch spun and walked out of the room, Alexander, Malena, and their crew on his heels. When they were out of sight, the sword hovering in front of Leaf clanked to the ground.

Taking Celyse into my arms, I hugged her to me, and Manny joined in. But our group hug didn't last long. The house shifted. The walls trembled. I pulled away from Celyse and stared at the ceiling, my mind instantly going to Draven because I knew what it was like to be in a house under his attack.

"Holy hell," I uttered. "He said he wouldn't harm us, but he said nothing about harming the house."

"And we are in the house," Celyse mumbled.

"It's his signature move!" Manny yelled.

A blast crashed against the structure, followed by another and another. I knew it was Draven's fiery magic. I could picture him outside flinging his red energy at us. What had I done?

"I told you!" Leaf spat.

Jaid and Leto looked at each other. "I will check the back," Leto shouted.

"I will check the front," Jaid called.

Rook, Ferna, and Parlan dashed off to help too. I bolted for the back windows, tossing chairs out of the way. Manny, Celyse, and Leaf joined me. We banged and kicked the glass, but everything was sealed shut, no doubt by Draven's magic.

Jaid and Leto skidded back into the room.

"There's no way out!" Jaid yelled as more crashing reverberated through the walls. This time, the force sent cracks running across the ceiling like crooked tendrils.

A woman in a red dress ran into the room. "Hurry! Follow me!"

"Lady Wren!" Celyse called out.

"Come!" she ordered, taking off out of the room.

Celyse signaled me with a nod, then shouted, "Follow Lady Wren!"

She dashed after the tall fae woman, and everyone followed. We sprinted down a long hallway, the walls creaking with each step, and emerged into an expansive stone kitchen. Chunks of plaster and tufts of dust sprinkled from the ceiling as the walls began cracking in every direction. Beyond a huge counter and a wood stove was a large set of shelves that had been swung open like a door. A line of staff in white uniforms were rushing through.

"A tunnel system!" Celyse said. Just like the one in the Strong Haven East palace.

"Yes," the woman replied, standing by the opening and ushering everyone through. "Hurry, hurry."

Jaid darted up to her. "You go!" he ordered. "I will see everyone through!"

She ducked in after the last staff person. Then Jaid took over. He grabbed Manny's shirt and shoved him in. Celyse and I were next, followed by the others.

The earth shook and split with each step, slamming us from side to side against the dirt walls as we lumbered forward. In the distance, a torchlight bobbed about, and behind us, light from the kitchen still shone.

I kept my hand on Celyse's shoulder and my eye on Manny, praying we'd make it out, when an explosion blasted all around us. The force pummeled into my back, and we tumbled to the ground in a heap, the light sources around us snuffing out.

"Is everyone okay?" I hollered.

"Yes," Celyse sputtered with a cough.

"I'm okay!" Manny hollered.

"Up, up! Keep going!" Lady Wren called from somewhere ahead of us.

We were running out of time. I pulled Celyse to her feet, staying close to her as we pushed forward. Finally, a spot of daylight came into view. Small at first, it grew in brightness until we were under a tunnel opening. A stocky dwarf was kneeling, boosting everyone to the surface.

"Climb!" He hollered.

The dwarf hoisted Manny first, then Celyse, and then me. I scrambled out of the opening, then surveyed my surroundings, the sight shocking me to my core. The structure had collapsed to the ground in a pile of bricks, wood, and debris and a billowing cloud of dust rose from the heap.

“Oh my God,” Manny uttered.

“A god did not do this,” Lady Wren snarled, tears in her eyes. “A demon witch named Draven did.”

Scanning the area, I saw that none of the carriages were around. Neither were our horses. It appeared Draven, Malena, and the others were gone too.

A boom shook the ground, like an earthquake. I grabbed Celyse and brought her close, shielding her with my arms, not knowing the source of the sound.

“The tunnel!” Rook shouted.

We ran back to the opening, but it had caved in. Rook, Jaid and Leto fell on all fours, clawing at the dirt. “There are still fae in there!” Rook yelled.

Taking in a quick assessment, I saw Ferna and Parlan were missing. My gut lurched as I dove in with everyone else, digging and pulling at the ground, frantically trying to find the opening. If this failed, everything would fall apart.

“Come on!” Leto yelled, desperation and anger in his face.

“Here!” Jaid called, uncovering a hand.

We flung out the dirt, exposing an arm, and then a head. It was Ferna. Leto lifted her and placed her on the ground. He worked fast, opening her mouth, swiping with his fingers to remove a clump of dirt. He alternated between blowing air and pumping her chest, his motions quick and steady.

Nearby, Parlan had been dug out and laid flat like Ferna, along with the bodies of two staff members. I got to work on Parlan, while Celyse worked on one of the small staffers, and Lady Wren on the other.

We worked for several long minutes, blowing and pressing, trying to bring life into the bodies. But nothing was working. It was Lady Wren who sat back first.

"They are gone," she uttered.

14
CELYSE

I stayed on my knees, staring at the motionless bodies in disbelief, my heart crying out for Ferna, Parlan, and the innocent staff members of Strong Haven West while my eyes watered over.

"It's all my fault," Manny muttered, wiping his face and hiding his tears. "I did this to them."

"Don't do that, Manny," Julio whispered.

"We all know whose fault it is," I added.

I rose to my feet, and so did Julio. He grasped my hand and moved in close to me. Manny joined us and we huddled together, not knowing what to do next.

Lady Wren sat back, but stayed close to the body she had been trying to revive. Her stare was up and away, her mind lost in her grief.

Leto stayed kneeling on the ground. He closed Ferna's eyelids with a gentle touch, then Parlan's. It took him a while to speak.

"Ferna and Parlan had a bakery in the human world, and a great life together. They only came back to Faevenly because I asked them to. They never wanted this. Not any of it. "

The heavy weight of sorrow hovered over all of us,

hanging so thick in the air it was hard to breathe, and I had only met Ferna and Parlan not long ago. I could only imagine how Leto was feeling.

Leto slowly rose to his feet. "Lady Wren, are any more of your folk missing?"

She nodded. "Lord Delfin is unaccounted for, as well as Winkle, the dwarf in the tunnel who was helping hoist others out."

"We dig all night," Leto said. "So we can properly honor the dead."

Leto and Jaid set Ferna and Parlan aside with care and attention, and we all got busy digging. With nothing but our hands to use as tools, we worked in concert at the dirt for hours until we finally found the two missing bodies. We lifted them out of the ground and lined them side by side.

Swiping my matted hair out of my face, I stared at their still forms. Earlier today, they were preparing for a meeting of dignitaries. Now they were no longer alive. I knew Manny thought he was to blame, and I had said Draven was; but really, everything was my fault.

If I had not found that shimmer, none of this would have happened.

"What do we do now?" Manny asked in a hushed tone.

Leto wiped his brow with his sleeve. "We take them into the woods so that they may return to nature, where they belong. From there, they will journey to the Passing Place."

Taking care with the bodies, we carried them one by one into the woods, to a small clearing surrounded by flowering trees. Lady Wren knelt on the ground and worked on Lord Delfin. She combed back his long silver hair with her fingers, then removed the dirt that had settled into the creases of his eyes. With his hair and face perfectly prepared, she smoothed out his long red coat, straightened his lapel, and dusted off his pants. He wasn't wearing any boots, and I wondered what had happened to them.

The maid servants conducted the same sort of preparation with Winkle and the other two staffers, cleaning the dirt from their small faces and arranging their hair. They also dusted off their clothes until they looked perfect, as if they were merely resting in a field.

The hardest part was watching Leto tend to Ferna and Parlan. Declining our offers to help him, he took to the task on his own.

He removed every trace of dust and dirt from their faces. Starting at their foreheads, he made gentle swiping motions across their skin, then moved his fingertips with precision and care over their eyes, down their noses, from cheek to cheek, and then finally to their chins.

With that finished, he turned his attention to their clothing. He brushed off their shirts, belts, and pants until not a speck of dirt remained. The last remaining detail was their hair. He worked their braided locks with his fingers, making sure each strand was in place and clean and smooth.

"I am so very sorry, my friends," he said to them. "So very sorry."

With the bodies prepared, Lady Wren and the maid servants went to the nearby gardenia bushes. Following their lead, the rest of us did the same, and we all plucked the white blooms. With our arms full, we went back and placed the fragrant flowers around the bodies.

With the sun setting and the air cooling, we took turns saying goodbye. And when everyone was finished, we went back to the rubble, where we found our horses had returned.

A small maid servant said, "See? Our friends are already doing good works for us."

Lady Wren managed a smile. "I suppose they are. And now that they have passed, we must do right by them and seek justice for their shortened lives. Draven, Malena, and Alexander cannot get away with what they have done here."

I nodded. "They most assuredly will not, Lady Wren. You have my word."

Before we could discuss our next steps, a lone rider on a white steed came into view, galloping our way.

"What is this?" I asked.

"I do not know, but I suggest we prepare for anything," Jaid said.

We gathered together, strength in numbers, and waited for the rider to get close. Galloping at top speed, with his long silver hair flowing behind him, he began slowing when he neared.

He eyed us each in turn as his steed circled us, then kept his stare on me as he came to a full stop. "I come from Cuesta with a note for Princess Celyse."

He held out a rolled parchment. Was I still a princess? Exchanging a look with Julio, I advanced slowly to get it. When it was in my grasp, the rider spurred the horse around and took off the way he had come.

Everyone closed in around me. I broke the Lind seal and unscrolled the document. I read out loud. "House Lind is prepared to support Lady Celyse upon the removal of Draven the witch and Usurper Malena. Signed, Lord Lind."

I lowered the note, staring at everyone with surprise. "The tides are changing," I said, suddenly filled with hope.

Julio grabbed my hand and smiled. But it was Manny who spoke. "It's about damn time."

"There will be no resting on our laurels," Lady Wren admonished, dampening the moment with a heavy dose of reality. "There is still much to do."

According to Lady Wren, there was a small village two hours to the east by horseback. Though night had quickly descended on us, there were plenty of stars in the sky to light our way.

With nothing but a few weapons we had found scattered about, and the clothes on our backs, we trotted at an easy pace. Manny ended up riding behind Julio and surprisingly kept quiet as we rode. One of the maid servants rode with me. As I trotted, I kept my horse close to Julio's. I never wanted to part from him again.

Even though a sliver of hope had settled inside of me with the offer from House Lind, it could not compare to the despair I still carried. Draven had brought down the Strong Haven West Manor with a mind to kill us, and Malena was fine with that. Yet somehow we had managed to come out only losing six souls. While six was still too many, I was grateful for those that had been spared.

But I also could not help but wonder who we would lose next.

15
MALENA

I stared out the opening of the carriage as we sped away from Strong Haven West, watching as Draven stood outside the manor house, flinging fiery red blasts of magic at the structure. He hurled with frightening intensity, each movement of his arms and hands rapid and furious. Even though I sat safely in my ride, I crouched back a little, as if his magic would somehow bounce back and obliterate us like bugs.

"I have never seen such a thing," I murmured, terrified, my hand resting over my pounding heart.

"Nor have I," Alexander uttered, gazing out the opening with me.

With each assault, the the structure swayed, like a tree in the wind, until it tumbled down in a heap of smoky debris.

I pulled away from my lookout, dumbfounded, and pressed my back against the carriage seat. My fingers dug into the thick velvet fabric of the bench as my gut twisted at the thought of Celyse and the others being smashed by all the brick and stone.

Stealing my resolve, I reminded myself that whatever happened to them was their doing, not mine.

Alexander took my hand. "It will be well, my love."

I kept my chin up, determined to be strong no matter what, the way Mother had taught me. "I know." But then my thoughts turned to the direness of my situation. The council had not been able to approve my elevated status. I shifted and faced Alexander. "I was not approved."

"Nothing to worry about," he soothed. "You do not technically need anyone's approval to step into a role that is properly yours. The whole pomp and circumstance of a big gathering is really for show."

I blinked, finding comfort in his words. "You think so?"

"I know so. I have talked at length with my father about it. He says the meetings for succession do not change anything. You are the High Queen. I will be High King. No one will challenge us."

Like the other royals that had raced off to their homesteads, Alexander's father had gone to High Meadow, so I could not confirm with him. But I knew Alexander spoke the truth. He wanted his position as much as I wanted mine.

I cupped his face with my hands and stared into his adoring eyes. "You are so wise, my love. Together we are the perfect couple. Powerful, intelligent, and above everyone else."

He took my hand and kissed my palm, then trailed his lips up my arm, but I was not ready for affection. I wanted to continue strategizing and planning. There would be time for kissing and the like later.

I pulled my arm away. “We still have province business to discuss, Alexander.”

He sat back. “Of course.”

“Did you speak to the other members of the provinces before my arrival? You had said in your note that Cuesta and Summit Range might not be standing with me, and that you were going to Cuesta.”

“I did go to Cuesta before arriving here. Unfortunately, they were noncommittal. I did not have a chance to speak to Summit Range. Sand Bluff, on the other hand, assures me of their loyalty. I had a chance to chat with them before you arrived.”

“Well, that is good.”

“It is. As for Cuesta, we simply need to find something to entice them. It makes no matter what Summit Range does, as they will be outnumbered.”

I tilted my head and stared at him for a minute. “Entice?”

“You know, something they need that only we can give them. Like promises and favors. Or even stature. Something to secure their loyalty.”

I rubbed my temples, my head starting to pound. “Is it not enough that I have Draven doing my bidding? And with High Meadow and Sand Bluff standing with Strong Haven, can we not just use a show of force against Cuesta and Summit Range? I mean, why do we need to give anyone anything? Especially when they do not deserve it?”

“I suppose we could simply issue orders. Three against two always wins,” he said.

"Exactly." I snuggled into him, not wanting to talk anymore about provinces or favor or Draven or the devastation at Strong Haven West. I only wanted to be Malena with Alexander—two lovers ruling the world, ensuring the peace and safety of our kingdom, and triumphing over evil . . . together . . .

I sat up with a start, an idea sparking within me. "Alexander, I know what we should do."

He raised a brow. "What?"

"Let us perform the binding ceremony as soon as we get back to the east. No guests. No preparations. Simply two soul mates of the most powerful houses joining together forever. No one will ever challenge us when we are one united force, and together we will rule Faevenly."

He cupped my face with his strong hands. "Nothing would please me more, my love."

Our lips met, and in that moment nothing else mattered but me, Alexander, and our power.

16
CELYSE

We traveled in silence, all of us needing time to grapple with the collapse of Strong Haven West and the loss of our friends. At least, I knew I did. The fact that Malena could have allowed something like that to happen sickened me. And the idea that she and Draven and Alexander were probably celebrating my death left me hollow. The sheer magnitude of her evil soared beyond my wildest comprehension. Her wickedness even rivaled her mother's. But she always was a perfectionist.

My thoughts also dwelled on Julio. My heart had been calling for him since our separation, every part of me longing for us to be reunited. But now, all that had been ruined. I could see in his face that he blamed himself for what had happened. But he had done the right thing trading Manny. We all would have done the same. With no other viable choice, and standing against an evildoer like Draven, the situation would have ended up with someone's death no matter what. There was no way we would have come out of the manor unscathed. I needed to tell him that.

"There," Lady Wren called out after a while,

pointing at a dim light in the distance. "We will find safe haven there. It is an inn owned and operated by a friend."

The village was the smallest I had ever seen, if it even was a village. A handful of simple and plain structures of brick and stone with flat roofs lined a narrow road. With the hour so late, everyone appeared to have turned in for the night. The only place with light still burning was at the end of the pass, where we were heading, at a somewhat larger structure that stood out from the rest.

We left our horses together, then gathered in front of the simple wooden door. Lady Wren knocked, and a small fae with long red hair and bright green eyes opened the door.

She smiled. "Lady Wren. What a pleasant surprise. It is lovely to see you."

"And you, Lady Pen."

Lady Pen looked over our group with curiosity. She spotted me right away and let out a startled gasp. "A daughter of Strong Haven."

It seemed the tiny village had no idea what had been happening in Strong Haven. Instead of catching her up on how I had fallen from grace and lost my status, I offered a nod. "It is nice to make your acquaintance. You may call me Celyse."

Her eyes sparkled with delight. "Thank you, Celyse. You may call me Pen."

Pen scanned our faces with stitched brows, clearly realizing something was amiss. She brought her attention back to Lady Wren. "How may I help you and your companions?"

"If possible, we require lodgings for the night, should you have the space for us," she said.

"Of course. There are no other visitors, so there is plenty of space." Pen swung open the door and stepped aside, motioning for us to enter. "Please, you are all welcome."

We shuffled in and found ourselves in a quaint sitting room with a stone floor, stone walls, a long bench, a low table in the middle, and wooden chairs on either side. A fireplace nestled in the corner of the room with a cozy blaze burning. The smell of cinnamon and cloves permeated the air.

"I am honored to have you all," she said. "You may roam freely and help yourselves to anything you wish. There are three unoccupied bedchambers for your choosing. The washing facilities are outside in the back."

"This is more than adequate, thank you Pen," Lady Wren said.

"You are most welcome." Her eyes lingered on Leto for a few seconds before she added, "I will fetch some food and drink."

She disappeared, leaving me and the others alone. We stood around, as if unsure of what to do next. As someone used to running a manor house, it did not take Lady Wren long to assume her regular role.

"The staff and I will take one of the bedchambers. The rest of you can split up however you wish amongst the remaining two." She motioned the staffers to follow her. "We have had a long hard day and will turn in for the night."

She and the maid servants left, and my mind went to the sleeping arrangements. Before I could even bring it up, Leto piped in. "Celyse will take one room, the rest of us will manage in the other."

Rook crossed his arms. His dark, penetrating eyes hung heavy with exhaustion, and maybe even pain. "I will take my rest outside, but first, we need a plan. I demand vengeance for the wrongdoings of Strong Haven. Malena and those standing with her must be stopped." He slammed his fist against his open palm. "They must suffer for what they have done and continue to do to Sublanders and humans!"

Leaf joined Rook with fervor. "I agree. They must be dealt with."

"We all agree on that," Jaid chimed in. "Their crimes extend much further than the fae realm."

Pen came back into the room, and everyone hushed. She looked about, noticing Lady Wren and the maid servants had left the room.

"They have retired for the evening," I explained.

"Understandable," she answered. "The hour is late." She set a pitcher of drink and a tray of food and cups on a table to the side. She filled one of the cups with water and handed it to Leto.

He smiled at her, and I thought I detected a look of fancy in his eye. "Thank you, Lady Pen," he said.

"You are most welcome . . ." She paused a moment, as if waiting for him to say something else. "Leto," he offered, catching on to her pause. "You may call me Leto."

She blushed. "Leto." Then, as if remembering there were others in the room, she cleared her throat. "I will see you all in the morning."

After she left, Manny leaned in. "Dude," he said to Leto in a hushed voice. "That was a love connection if I ever did see one."

"Enough, Manny," Leto admonished.

"I'm just saying," Manny said. He perused the offerings. "Well, I could use some refreshments."

He served himself some drink and grabbed a few pieces of bread. I was not hungry, and it seemed no one else was either, as everyone shuffled around, settling in for a discussion. I made my way to the bench and took a seat. Julio stood next to me. Jaid and Leto set their bows and quivers on the ground, then sat on the wooden chairs. The Sublanders, Rook and Leaf, remained standing together by the door.

Jaid rubbed his forehead. "I know how to fight. I know how to gather forces. But I do not know how to face the likes of Draven. How do we strike a witch? His evil knows no bounds."

"I wish I knew," Leto answered.

My mind took me back to Strong Haven West, picking apart everything that had happened, when Leaf's exchange with the elder Lord Kane popped to mind.

I turned to the young fae. "You know the elder Lord Kane. He referred to you by name."

Leaf shuffled his stance, a look of anger covering his face.

"I was meaning to get to that," Leto added, turning to face Leaf.

"As was I," Jaid chimed in.

Leaf crossed his arms. "My business is my own. It does not concern any of you."

Julio tilted his head at the fae, studying him. "We are connected in all this, like it or not. So, if there's something we need to know, then you need to tell us."

"And who are you?" Leaf spat, coming up to Julio. "The all-powerful human witch who can do actually nothing?"

Julio shoved him, banging him against the wall. Leaf flared his nostrils and charged, but Leto was quick to jump in the middle.

"He is with us," Leto warned Leaf, straining as he held the fae back. "That is who he is. And he can do way more than you. I have seen it."

The last thing I wanted was a fight, especially in the home of a welcoming friend of Lady Wren's. We could not risk being cast out. "Please, stop," I pleaded. "We have a common enemy, and if we are to defeat that common enemy, we need to band together."

"Sorry," Julio said, combing his fingers through his hair and walking away.

I put my hand on Julio's arm and brought him back

to the bench with me. I gave everyone some time to calm down before I continued with my questioning.

"Leaf, how does Lord Kane know you?"

Leaf moved away from everyone and pressed his back against the wall. "He knows me because I am a Kane."

A piece of bread fell out of Manny's mouth. It bounced off his leg and tumbled to the floor. "Uh, what?" His eyes darted around. "Kane is like, a bad guy, right?"

My eyes stayed on Leaf, the similarities between him and Alexander coming into view. Same jet-black hair, same tall and slender build, and same blue eyes. The only real difference between them was that Leaf had full lips, whereas Alexander's were thin.

"You are a Kane?" I asked in a disbelieving tone. "Alexander is your brother?"

"Explain," Leto demanded. "Before we cast you out."

Leaf crossed his arms. "My father bedded a human, and I was born," he said simply and abruptly. He sneered at Leto. "Or would you like an explanation of the act?"

Leto was about to rise to his feet, but Jaid stopped him with a shake of his head. "It is not worth it, brother," he muttered.

"That is right, Leto," Leaf laughed. "I am not worth anything."

"Stop it, Leaf," I called out, suddenly feeling sorrow for him because I knew exactly how he felt. With his revelation swirling in my head, I said, "You are like me."

"Ha," Leaf scoffed. "No, princess. I am nothing like you. I was not raised in a palace, or given status, or held out as a full-blooded fae. I never had riches or servants doing my bidding." He slammed his fist against his chest. "I was cast out as a child and sent to the Sublands to fend for myself. If not for Rook and the Caileans, I would have died!"

He breathed heavily from all the emotion, and a sharp twinge of pity for him settled inside of me. I could not blame him for his anger. He must have endured much pain. If not for the High Queen being with child and she and my mother delivering at the same time, I do not know if my story would have been the same. I may have been cast out too. Or even killed.

Jaid spoke. "One province kept their half-blooded fae; the other did not. I suspect every province has an illegitimate child or two."

"It would not surprise me in the least," Leto said. "Royals have deep secrets."

Leaf shifted his weight and clasped his hands behind his back. He exchanged a look with Rook. A look that meant he wanted to say something more but was not sure if he should.

"Go on," Rook encouraged Leaf. "Tell them."

All eyes swung to Leaf.

"Tell us what?" I asked.

In a lowered voice, Leaf said, "Royals have deep secrets. But so do witches."

Jaid raised his brow. "Witches?"

"Yes, witches," Leaf repeated. He leaned in, as if what he was about to say could not be overheard. "Draven spends a great deal of time in the Sublands. Always has. As a trusted advisor to the High King and High Queen of Strong Haven, it is his appointed duty to oversee the aquoise mining operation. But I think his visits mean something more."

"I'm confused," Julio cut in. "What is aquoise?"

I forgot that I had learned out about the blue rock when Julio and I were apart and had not had a chance to tell him. I explained, "Aquoise is a rock found only in the Sublands that gives finite unnatural strength. The Strongs took control of it after the Sublanders discovered it, and used humans to mine it."

"Wait a second," Manny said. "The blue rock we mined after we broke out of those cages turns users into Avengers?"

"Really, Manny?" Julio said, tossing his friend a look.

He shrugged, as if it were the most normal question to ask, and I wondered what an avenger was.

"Manny, please focus," Leto murmured. He pinched the bridge of his nose. "Continue, Leaf."

Leaf scooted in. "I have seen Draven go into the mines and stay there longer than anyone has ever stayed. Sometimes days on end. A few times I went in after he left, to see where he had been, but could find not any trace of him. It was as if he went in . . . and vanished . . . and then came back out."

"Vanished?" Manny whispered, his eyes larger than usual.

I glanced at Julio, and we exchanged a questioning look. I brought my attention back to Leaf. "Do you know what he was doing?"

Leaf shook his head. "I do not."

"What is down there?" Leto mused out loud, bringing his hands together and steepling his fingers. "What is Draven up to?"

"Aquoise," Rook said. "Aquoise is down there."

Leto continued tapping his fingers. "Correct, but why would an all-powerful witch need aquoise, especially if the effect of the rock is finite?"

We had spent a good amount of time with Leaf in the caves, and I wondered why he was only now revealing vital information. "Why did you not say something when we were down there together?" I asked.

"I did not know you or trust you," Leaf said. "And if you must know, I still do not trust you. I am only saying something now because Rook trusts you."

Leto began pacing, rubbing his chin. "Draven is the key to all of this. Everything. He holds the power, not the Strongs." He glanced at me. "Who knows? Maybe he always has. The last High Queen and Draven were nearly inseparable. I wonder if Malena is merely his plaything, like a toy."

Julio rubbed the back of his neck. "I feel it too. He is controlling everything."

"Whoa," Manny said, facing Julio. "Feel it feel it? Or . . . witchy feel it?"

"Leto is right," Jaid said, ignoring Manny. "If we can eliminate Malena's witch, then it will be much easier to take her down."

"Okay, so what does that mean?" Manny asked, cringing as though he knew the answer and was not going to like it.

"It means we go back to the Sublands," Jaid answered. "At first light. We must figure out Draven's connection to the mines."

"Know your enemy," Julio added.

Leto nodded. "That's right."

Manny shot up to his feet. "No, no, no, no. Are y'all crazy?" He spun around to Julio. "You weren't there, dude, but there are these crazy whispering winds in those tunnels that try to kill people!" He pointed at himself. "Like me! I'm people! And I was almost killed!"

Julio put his hands on Manny's shoulders. "It's okay. You don't have to go in."

"Really?" His shoulders relaxed some, but the look of terror on his face remained. "Because I feel like I-I-I can't go through that again."

"The fewer we have in the cave tunnels, the better, anyway," Leto said, solidifying Manny's desire to stay.

Not that I could blame Manny at all. Those winds almost had him.

"Agreed," Jaid said. "The Sublands are under Malena's rule. It will take skill and stealth to get back in those caves. We cannot have any distractions. Anyone who does not want to go in should wait outside the village."

"Leaf and I will not be going in either," Rook announced. "We will most assuredly be spotted and will jeopardize the mission. We will wait outside the village with Manny."

A sigh of relief escaped Manny. "Yeah, good idea. I can stay with Rook and Leaf."

Jaid assessed everyone in the room, his stare landing on me to see if I had anything to add, but I did not. His plan was solid. I nodded to let him know.

"It is settled," Jaid said. "Julio, Celyse, Leto, and I will go into the tunnels; Manny, Rook, and Leaf will wait outside the village."

Rook moved away from the wall and to the door. "With that settled, I will retire outside for the evening."

"Me too," Leaf said.

With them gone, Manny was next to take his leave. "Well," he said with a giant yawn. "I'm exhausted." He got up and hesitated a few seconds for Julio.

"I'll be there later," Julio said to Manny.

With a nod, Manny left the room. Jaid and Leto retrieved their things and followed.

With everyone gone, I was finally alone with Julio. And I had much to say.

17

JULIO

I had wanted nothing more than to get back to Faevenly so I could save Manny and be with Celyse. But now others were dead because of me, and that was all I could think about as we planned to go to the Sublands in the morning.

When the room emptied, Celyse wrapped her hands around mine and pulled me down to the bench. She angled her body toward me. We sat like that a few long seconds before she spoke.

"You can talk to me, Julio."

"I know I can," I said, scooting closer to her, our knees touching. She tilted her head, her dark streak of hair spilling a bit into her eyes. I brushed it back but didn't say anything; I didn't know what to say. I felt weak and worthless.

She stroked my hand. "Are you going to tell me what you are thinking? I feel a heaviness from you."

I blew out. "Well, I'm no match for Draven, and I got six others killed. That pretty much sums it up." A lump formed in my throat as the lifeless images of Ferna, Parlan, and the others sprang to mind. I swallowed it down and forced the visual from my mind. "I have no idea how to use my powers, let alone get us out of this mess."

She nodded with understanding. "Julio, what happened at Strong Haven West was going to happen. None of it was your fault. Understand? Draven is pure evil. In that moment, when he offered the exchange, we had to take it. There was no other move for us."

I knew she was right—I had to save Manny—but I still felt the guilt in my gut like a ton of bricks weighing me down so hard I felt sick. "I know. But it sucks, and I feel awful," I said in a hushed tone.

She squeezed my hand. "As for not knowing what to do, none of us know what to do. We can only continue doing what is just and right and trust that in the end that is enough."

I shook my head, unable to believe that. "Do you really think it will be enough? Because I don't know anymore."

She cast her eyes down for a few long seconds before bringing them back up to me. "Maid Rell taught me a lot of things. One thing she used to say all the time was that good always wins. Good is stronger than evil—it is a bright sun that breaks through the cloudiest day and the hardest rain that ends the longest drought." She sighed. "Of course, when she said good, I thought she was talking about Strong Haven. But now I see the truth. She meant me. And you. All of us." She held my hands tight. "We are the good, Julio. And I believe her words. One way or another, we will defeat Draven and those who stand with him."

The fact that Maid Rell was dead moved to the forefront of my mind. With everything happening so fast, we hadn't talked about her. "I'm so sorry about Maid Rell, Celyse. Sounds like she was pretty amazing."

Her eyes watered. "Thank you. She was."

I traced the side of her face with my fingertips. Everything about her drew me in. Her seductive emerald eyes. Her perfect pink lips. Her kiss was supposed to be deadly to humans, but we had managed to kiss at the Green Falls and I survived. I didn't know if it was because we were in the magical water, or if it was because she was half-human. In that moment, I was willing to risk everything to find out.

I leaned in. "Celyse, I want to try something."

She moved forward, her lips hovering before mine, when shuffling footsteps sounded. We separated quickly as Manny strode in.

His eyes widened when he saw us. "Oh, um . . . sorry." He pointed at the table with the food. "I was hungry."

I motioned at the food. "Help yourself."

He went to the table and filled his hands with as much bread as he could carry, tossed me a sheepish look, then went back to where he had come from.

Celyse smiled. "That Manny is a character."

I laughed, thinking that calling him a character didn't even cover it. "Yeah, he is."

With the mood ruined, we sat back a bit, neither one of us knowing what to say for a while.

"So," I said, inspecting her all-black pants and shirt and her weapons. It wasn't her usual royal attire. I ran my finger across the rough fabric of her pants. "This is a new look on you."

She looked down at herself and smiled. "Yes, it is. I call it my sword fighting outfit. I acquired it at a village." She pointed to the scabbard at her waist. "This is where my sword goes." She pointed to the sheath at her belt. "This is where I keep my dagger." She pointed to another pouch on her belt. "This is where I keep sleeping powder."

My brow raised as I eyed the small pouch. "Sleeping powder? What do you need that for?"

"You never know when you will need someone to go to sleep," she said with a smile.

"Well, your sword fighting outfit served you well today. You were really kicking ass with that sword. I had no idea you could fight like that."

She frowned. "I do not think I kicked anyone."

I chuckled, then shook my head. "It's an expression. It means you were doing a great job fighting."

"Oh," she said, lighting up at the compliment. "Thank you. It is one thing my father pressed upon me—to learn how to fight with daggers, swords, and hands. I have mastered the dagger and the sword but have yet to master hand-to-hand combat, though I have taken many classes."

"Can Malena fight like you?" I asked.

She scoffed. "No, she never wanted to learn."

I raised my hands like a boxer. "Well, I'm pretty

good with a good old-fashioned fist fight, but I can't do any of that other stuff."

She pulled my hands back to her and started playing with my fingers. "Maybe you can teach me what you can do, and I can teach you what I can do."

Her touch filled me with heat and desire, and I wanted nothing more than to kiss her all over. "I would love that."

"Our bodies would have to get close." She leaned forward, her eyes seductive and filled with longing, her spicy, floral scent driving me wild.

I scooted closer to her. "Like this?"

"More like this," she said, bringing one of her legs between mine so that our legs were threaded together.

I swallowed, nervous someone would walk in on us sitting so close. "Do you think we should maybe go—"

"To my bedchamber?"

I swallowed again. "Well, I was going to say take a walk, but yeah. We could go to your bedchamber. If that's okay with you, that is."

She stood, her hand still in mine, and pulled me to my feet. "It is okay with me."

She led me out of the small room and to the dark corridor. Rooms lined both sides, but only one had an open door with faint light glowing from within. We walked in, and she closed the door with a soft push.

The room had stone walls and a stone floor, like the front of the house. There was a small bed along one wall and a table holding a lantern, a bowl, and a pitcher along another wall. Celyse removed her weapons and placed them on the table, and I set my dagger with hers. She pulled me over to the bed and we sat down facing each other.

A rush of memories of us seeing each other through the shimmer in my bedroom flooded my mind. Except this time, we were together. In the flesh.

"You know what this reminds me of?" I asked.

She smiled. "The times I visited you through the shimmer."

"Yes," I laced my fingers through hers. "But now we're really together, and we can touch each other."

She moved my hand to her face and I cupped her cheek. She closed her eyes. "You do not even know how badly I wanted you to touch me all those times I came to you. It drove me mad."

I stroked her soft skin with my fingertips. "I felt the same way. I wanted you so bad it hurt."

My body burned for her, and I knew hers burned for me. I could feel her desire coming off her like a surge of heat filled with her sweet scent.

She opened her eyes. "I want more than anything to feel your lips on mine."

Pulsing waves of yearning coursed through me, sending my stomach tumbling. "Do you want to try?"

She sat back a little. She wrapped my hand in hers and held it to her. "If I hurt you, I would not be able to live with myself."

I studied her face, seeing the love and concern in her eyes, but also the deep longing. I could tell that even though she was scared, she wanted to try. And in that moment, I was ready to risk everything to be with her.

Scrambling for a theory on how we could be together, I said, "I think we were able to kiss before because you're half human, not because of the magic of the Green Falls. But I don't want you to do anything you're not comfortable with."

She squeezed my hand. "If you are willing, then I am."

I had never wanted someone the way I wanted Celyse. My body hungered for her. My heart and soul called to her, as if we were fated to be together, lovers from different realms brought together by destiny.

I swallowed, and whispered, "I'm willing."

She licked her lips and leaned forward. Inch by inch, we closed the gap between us. And ever so slowly, our lips met. I held the connection, savoring the softness of her touch, then brushed my lips softly across hers before breaking away.

Our eyes held on to each other, waiting for something to happen. Nothing did.

"You are still alive," she beamed.

I smiled, "I am."

She grabbed my shirt and yanked me to her. We connected again, this time with force and intensity. Our lips parted; our tongues intertwined. Her velvety smooth and delicious mouth drove me crazy as we devoured each other with passion and desperation. She laced her hands behind my neck and fell back on the bed, taking me with her.

"More, Julio. Give me more," she panted against my mouth.

I ran my mouth down her neck, kissing all the way to her collarbone, breathing her in and savoring her taste, not wanting to stop as she threaded her hands through my hair with a soft moan.

I lifted myself onto my arms and looked down at her. A soft pink flush colored her cheeks, and a sultry yearning filled her eyes.

"You are so beautiful," I whispered.

"As are you, my earthly god." She touched my lips with her fingers and trailed them down my neck, reaching the edge of my shirt and tugging it over my head. She placed her hands on my chest, caressing me softly.

"Oh, Celyse," I groaned. "You don't know what you're doing to me."

She drew in a breath, her lips parting as if words had suddenly failed her. "Take me, Julio. All of me." She exhaled shakily, her gaze holding mine as if the world had fallen away. "All that I am is yours."

"Are you sure?" I asked, searching her face for even a flicker of hesitation.

She edged up and slipped her shirt over her head, exposing her gorgeous body. "Yes," she breathed. "I am sure."

We spent the night exploring each other in every way possible, my mind and my senses drowning in her while my body connected with hers completely and intimately. She was mine, and I was hers.

Forever.

Celyse snuggled into me, her arm wrapped around my waist and her legs intertwined with mine. I held her to me, not wanting to let go, the soft glow from the lantern allowing me to study her gorgeous face and perfect body. But I knew I needed to get up before the others awoke. No one needed to know that Celyse and I had spent the night together. Though Manny, Jaid, and Leto probably knew since we were supposed to be sharing a room.

I kissed her earlobe, then whispered. "I need to get to the other room before someone wakes up."

She raised herself on her arm and watched as I slid out of the bed and slipped on my clothes. She smiled. "I love you, Julio."

I bent down and kissed her. "I love you too. But now I'm Julio? I'm not an earthly god anymore?"

A smile spread across her beautiful face. "You will always be my earthly god."

I smiled. "You will always be my fae princess."

Before I could change my mind about leaving, I quietly opened the door and tiptoed out. Closing the door softly so as not to make a sound, I turned and almost ran into Jaid. He was fully dressed, his quiver and bow strapped on, dagger at his waist and sword at his side. He held a lantern to light his way.

"Jaid," I said, startled.

He wore a blank expression and nodded. "Julio."

He continued down the corridor and to the main room where we had gathered earlier. Then Leto came out of a room, dressed and ready like Jaid.

"Julio," he said with a nod.

"Leto." I rubbed the back of my neck. "Why are you and Jaid up so early?"

"We plan to do some scouting before we leave." He motioned to the door he had emerged from. "Get some rest. We leave after daybreak."

"Yeah, okay," I said, completely exhausted. I entered the darkened room and fumbled around a bit before I bumped into a bed. I patted it and found it empty, then lay down and closed my eyes, my mind replaying every moment with Celyse until I drifted to sleep.

A SHAKING OF MY SHOULDERS WOKE ME UP.

"Hey," Manny said, followed by more shaking. "It's time to get up."

My eyes slitted open. Sunlight bathed the small room from a large window, and Manny's fro came into view. "What time is it?" I muttered.

"Early, and we're all getting ready to leave."

I sat up and rubbed the crust from my sleepy eyes. "Man, I was tired."

He wiggled his eyebrows. "When I fell asleep, you still weren't in the room. So what happened?"

Rubbing my face, I said, "Nothing happened." I shuffled my way over to the table with the bowl and pitcher. I poured the water in and started splashing my face. "Where is everybody?"

"Jaid and Leto did some scouting and just got back. They're prepping the horses now with Leaf and Rook. Celyse is in the kitchen packing up supplies. Pen and Lady Wren and the others are helping her."

The cool water on my face refreshed me, helping me fully awaken. "Where's Lady Wren going?" I asked.

"Nowhere. I think she's staying here."

"I see," I said. "Well, I'll go help them. But first I need to go to the restroom. I'll be right back."

"Out the front and to the right, behind the house," Manny called out.

Outside, I exchanged silent nods with Jaid, Leto, Rook, and Leaf as I went to the small building that was just like an outhouse. After doing my business, I went back to the house and to the kitchen.

Celyse's face lit up when she saw me. "Julio," she said. "Good morning."

I smiled. "Good morning."

Pen, Lady Wren, and Lady Wren's staff said good morning too as they busily worked in the stone and brick kitchen that smelled of bread and honey. Pen offered me a plate of biscuits with fruit and motioned to a small table with a stool.

"Thank you," I said. I sat and took a bite of the biscuit. Bursting flavors of rosemary and mint filled my mouth. "Wow, this is delicious."

Pen smiled. "Thank you. It is my mother's recipe. I am glad you like it."

I took another bite, then said, "Can I help with anything?"

"I am fine, but thank you for your offer," Pen said, moving about the kitchen with purpose.

Celyse sat on a stool across from me. She reached out and touched my arm, then said in a low voice, "Did you sleep well?"

"Incredibly well." I kissed her hand before anyone could notice. "And you?"

"The same. I am well rested," she said with a smile.

The sound of heavy boots pounded against the stone floor, and Leto entered the kitchen. "It is time to depart," he announced, keeping his gaze on Pen, as if nobody else were in the room.

Pen scooped up two cloth bags connected with a long rope. She passed the bags to Leto, letting her hand linger on his for a few seconds. "Drape these over your steed. There is enough bread to last you all a few days."

Leto gave her a half bow. "Thank you, Lady Pen."

Her eyes fluttered and her cheeks flushed. "You are most welcome, Leto. Perhaps you will come and see me again?"

He smiled and nodded, then took her hand and kissed her knuckles. "Nothing would please me more."

Celyse shot me a look of delight and surprise, and I couldn't help but smile. Pen had a thing for Leto, and the feeling was mutual.

We were ushered out to the front where the horses were, and I was relieved to see we had enough rides for each of us. Mounted and ready to go, we said our farewells to the group and galloped off.

With my horse next to Celyse's, my mind drifted to where we were going—the Sublands. Somehow or another, Celyse, Jaid, Leto, and I needed to find a way into the cave mines to figure out what Draven had been doing in there.

I hoped and prayed that whatever it was wouldn't get us killed.

18
MALENA

When we returned to Strong Haven, Alexander ushered me in safely, then took off for High Meadow to inform his mother and father of our upcoming binding and bring them back for a small ceremony.

Now, it was my turn to tell my mother about Alexander, along with the news of what had befallen Strong Haven West. I feared she would not be pleased to hear about losing the manor house. She loved visiting there and often went there for respite. But I hoped the news of my binding, which would solidify Strong Haven, would soften the blow. Mother always did appreciate a good arrangement.

Standing by my mother's bed, I did not say anything for a while. My disappointment over my situation had swept me away. Nothing could have prepared me for how I was to wed. I would not have a mother or father to perform the asking ceremony. Or an attendant sister to stand by my side. Or even a Great Hall filled with guests. Instead, the ceremony would simply consist of Alexander and me, Alexander's mother and father, a few members of the staff, and Lady Sonia as the presider. Draven could not enter the grounds but promised he would be nearby.

And it was all Celyse's fault.

"Mother," I said in a half whisper. "I have news about Alexander. But I suppose I should first tell you what happened at the Council of Five."

I perched myself on the edge of her bed and faced the large window. The curtains had been pulled back, allowing the daylight to swathe the room. The trees and shrubs beckoned me to go for a walk. For a second, I wished to be a carefree princess again, not a High Queen with trouble in the provinces. But my course was set, and I would not falter.

Forcing myself to be strong, I kept my stare on the maple trees. "Celyse and her band of traitors were at the Council of Five before I arrived. Fighting broke out. Fortunately, Draven showed up to assist. The human witch had me in his grasp, but devious Draven used trickery of words, and they released me in exchange for a measly human."

I glanced at her stern face. "Is that not absurd, Mother?" I scoffed. "Trading me for a hideous lesser being?" A laugh escaped my lips at the foolishness of it all.

"Anyway, Draven trapped them inside the manor house and brought the whole structure down on their heads. Celyse and her despicable humans and the traitors that stood with them are no longer." Then I muttered under my breath, "they all deserved it."

I studied her motionless face, hoping for any kind

of reaction, but got none. Regardless, I was sure of her agreement with me.

"Losing the manor house was a small price to pay for their removal. And I promise to rebuild for you, Mother. I will spare no effort. The new house will be grand and beautiful and will most assuredly meet your impeccable high standards." Picturing all the marble and gold and silver brought a smile to my face. "You will see," I muttered. "It will be the envy of all."

I imagined the scene in my head. I would vacation in the west, with a full entourage of staff. Anytime a dignitary called, their jaws would drop at the sight of the newest and grandest manor house. It was all I could do to focus on my conversation.

"As for Alexander and me, we have decided to have the binding performed right away, tomorrow in fact. He is off to bring his family here. We love each other, of course, and thought it best to solidify Strong Haven's place as soon as possible. With House Kane beside us, we will be invincible."

I glanced at Mother's thin lips, knowing that if she could she would smile at my cunning strategy. "I have planned a simple yet elegant color scheme of silver and purple. Maid Gidna has promised to have the Great Hall sparkling with perfection. She is also hard at work with the other maid servants fashioning a magnificent gown for me. And Flourish, the pixie, has been summoned to paint my face. Is that not grand? I will be more beautiful than the sun, the moon, and the stars themselves."

Studying her profile I added softly, "More beautiful than even you. No one will ever rival me. No one."

My chest swelled with pride at how amazing I was sure to look, and I almost wished the ceremony were this evening. But tomorrow would be here soon enough, and there was much to do.

I placed my hand on hers. "I am resilient, Mother. And it is all because of you. I am so grateful for you and everything you have taught me. Thank you, Mother."

THE DAY WENT ON WITH MUCH FUSS AND PREPARATION IN anticipation of the binding. The meal servants split into two groups to prepare for the dinner. Half of them sliced and cubed the finest cheeses from our cheese grotto and the ripest fruits from our garden. The other half got to work on baking bread, and soon the aroma of buttery wheat and herbs filled the cook room, trickling out into the main parts of the palace.

With the food underway, another team of maid servants busily cleaned and scrubbed every inch of the palace, making sure each room had an array of freshly cut flowers.

As for the gnomes, they were instructed to prune and tidy the gardens with the utmost care. Water features were to be spread out all along the back gardens, and I specifically instructed them to let loose a bevy of doves at the exact moment of the binding.

Before I knew it, the night came and went. And with much anticipation, my special day had arrived. I was determined to revel in it.

Like she did each day, Maid Gidna swept into my room, placed her tray of water on my side table, and pulled open my curtains. This time, she did not need to prod me out of bed. My excitement had me on my feet in a flash as I twirled with delight. I did not need a full audience to feel special. I only needed Alexander and his mother and father.

Maid Gidna smiled, clearly as delighted as me. "Today is your day, my High Queen!"

"It is, Gidna." She handed me a crystal glass filled with rose water and I took a few sips. "Is there any word from Alexander or his family this morning?"

"Yes, High Queen. He and the Lord and Lady of High Meadow arrived late last night. Windon ushered them to the guest house, and they have been there since."

I clapped my hands. "Oh, good. Please make sure they have whatever they wish. I want our guests comfortable and satisfied."

She bowed low. "Of course. They brought a full staff for their own convenience, but I have also sent them a few of our own. I assure you they will have everything they need."

I nodded, thinking she was turning out to be just as good, if not better, than that dreadful Maid Rell. I made a mental note to reward her with an extra bottle of special oils. I was sure she would like that.

With a smile, I handed her my emptied glass and slipped on my robe, ready to make my way to my dressing chamber. Before leaving, I paused and took a final look at the room where I had spent the last eighteen years, thinking how I was ready to leave all this behind, especially the memories I had made here with a traitorous half-sister who was now dead.

As High Queen of Faevenly and Lady of Strong Haven, I would be moving into the royal bedchamber, along with Alexander. Mother would be moved to different quarters, but still looked after with care and respect.

I hoped she would understand.

"Is something the matter?" Gidna asked.

"No," I answered, pulling my gaze away from the room and sweeping my thoughts aside. "All is well."

My dressing chamber normally buzzed with activity in the mornings. But this morning, it was doubly so. A harpist strummed a romantic tune in the corner, and a trio of maid servants scurried about, preparing my bath. They had brought in a gold-trimmed tub, which had lilacs and roses floating on the water. Steam hovered over the top, promising a warm and relaxing soak.

The smallest maid servant came to me and took my robe and nightdress. Feeling glorious, I carefully climbed into the luxurious pool and slid down so the water came to my chin. The maid set my things away, then held a pillow for me to rest my head, while another placed sliced cucumber on my eyes.

"Do you think I will be lovely?" I asked.

"Oh, yes indeed. You will be so lovely, High Queen," she said in her small voice.

Visions of myself radiating with queenly pride and wearing the most spectacular dress filled my mind, and I smiled. "I know."

As I lay there, one of the maids washed my long hair with a paste made of shea butter, coconut oil, and rose. Another took a cloth and scrubbed my body with aloe leaf juice, sunflower seed oil, and grapefruit.

After staying in the tub a good long while, I climbed out and stood while the maid servants dried my body. Then they slathered me with a lotion of lanolin and hibiscus. Feeling radiant and fresh, I raised my arms as they slipped a silk white underdress over my head and led me to a plush seat for primping.

Maid Gidna worked on my long silver locks, brushing and working them with oils until each strand resembled sparkling silver. She pinned the hair up with pearl fasteners, letting several loose strands fall to frame my face.

When she was finished, a light tapping sounded at the door. Maid Gidna dashed over to answer it, and in flew Flourish with a spectacular swoop.

"I am here, High Queen!" she announced in her melodious high-pitched voice, looking dazzling and excited.

Her short-cropped hair was purple the last time I saw her, like her wings, but this time both were pink. Even the leaves of red and gold that had strategically covered her green body were now leaves of orange and yellow.

"I love your new coloring," I said, admiring the flawless creature.

"Thank you, High Queen. I am honored to receive such a compliment from you." She brought her hand to her delicate face for a moment before saying, "May I commence my preparations?"

"You may, Flourish," I said with delight. "Make me the most beautiful maiden in all of Faevenly."

She batted her eyelashes. "Of course, High Queen."

I closed my eyes, not wanting to see anything until she finished, and she got to work. She flitted about as she painted my face with precision and grace. Her tiny fingertips tapped all over my skin, working on my forehead, my cheeks, my eyes, my lips, and even my chin.

When she finished, she flew around my head, circling a few times, then said, "you may open your eyes now."

Peeking ever so slowly, Flourish dipped out of the way so Maid Gidna could hold up the face mirror. And what I saw stunned me in the most amazing way.

I was beyond beautiful.

"Wow," I uttered, delighting at the perfect rosy cheeks, dramatic and deep purple hues on the eyelids, and the most majestic lilac on the lips. I knew Alexander would love it, but a twinge of sorrow struck me at all the royals who would be missing my event. They would never be able to see me like this.

"Does my work meet with your approval?" Flourish asked, flitting back into view.

"It does. Thank you so very much." And then I had a thought. "Flourish, will you please do me the honor of attending my binding ceremony?"

She blushed and bowed low. "I would love to, my High Queen. But alas, I have an engagement already this afternoon. My sincerest apologies."

My heart sank a little that she would not able to attend. "That is all right." And then I offered quickly, "Perhaps you can come to an event another time, then."

"Most assuredly, High Queen." She scanned my face one more time, flitting to and fro, from cheek to cheek, then asked, "If all is well with my artwork, may I take my leave now?"

I took another long look at myself, making sure I did not need any other attention, then said. "Yes, all is well. You make take your leave."

"Thank you, High Queen." She spun into a pirouette and buzzed out the window and away. I turned my attention back to my face, enraptured with my appearance, thinking of Alexander and how he would react to seeing me.

"High Queen," Maid Gidna said with excitement. "Your dress has arrived."

I clapped my hands together. "Wonderful!"

The door opened, and in came four maid servants, two on each side. They ushered in a purple dress made from the shiniest silk I had ever seen.

They stood on stools and held it up, revealing a plunging neckline lined with sparkling crystals. They spun it around, revealing a low back with the same crystal edging. A high slit on the side was also edged with the same crystal and would showcase my smooth leg. It was the perfect blend of royal and sexy.

"Maid Gidna," I uttered, my mouth nearly hanging open. "It is stunning."

She beamed, and so did the other maid servants. "I am so glad, High Queen. The dress is fashioned of mulberry silk, which is made from the cocoons of the Bombyx mori moth silkworms, which are fed only mulberry leaves. The resulting fabric is the softest in all of Faevenly. We were fortunate to have found this so quickly."

I held my hands together, overwhelmed with delight and joy. "Fortune favors me today," I announced, not even believing my luck at having everything prepared so perfectly and on such short notice.

I stood, ready for the donning of the dress. The maid servants pushed their stools closer, stepped up, and carefully placed the dress over my head. I threaded my arms through the opening, then shimmied as the buttery soft, shiny, luxurious material fell seamlessly into place. I walked to the floor-to-ceiling mirror and swayed back and forth, admiring my ample cleavage and tiny waist, knowing Alexander would be most pleased.

"Are you ready for your slippers and your oils?" Maid Gidna asked.

"I am ready."

She placed the most delicate crystal shoes in front of me, and I slipped them on with ease. Another maid servant held out a tray of oils. My hands hovered over the vials, my thoughts taking me to Celyse for a few seconds, but I dismissed her memory with a frown. How dare she invade my thoughts on my wedding day.

"The one in the middle is made of lilac, gardenia, and roses," the smallest maid servant said. "It is quite romantic, the way you like."

I plucked the delicate silver vial from the tray and opened it, wafting it under my nose. It was powdery, floral, and most definitely romantic.

"Perfect," I said, dabbing it on my wrists and behind my ears, and even swiping a droplet in my bosom.

"And now," Maid Gidna announced, "for the placement of the ceremonial crown." She gestured at the door, and a tall, muscular, silver-haired guard marched in carrying a black velvet pillow. On top sat the queen's crown. Tall and impressive, it was made of dazzling crystals and pearls with thin white intertwining branches.

Finally mine. My heart pattered at the sight of it, as I had yet to wear the ornamental jeweled headdress denoting my new status. I reached out with shaky hands and placed it on my head. It fit perfectly, as if crafted only for me.

Staring at myself in the mirror, I looked every part the High Queen, and I was ready to bind myself to Alexander. We would rule Faevenly with wisdom and force, his house and mine. Together forever.

Mother would be so proud.

"And Alexander's crown is downstairs?" I asked.

"Yes, High Queen," the guard answered. "It will be ready for placement after the binding."

"Very good," I said.

Exiting the dressing chamber, I was met by Windon. He nodded, stifling what was most assuredly a swallow of desire, then followed behind me. With slow and graceful steps, and with my head held high, I walked the long corridor to the stairwell and made my way down to the Great Hall.

The room was bathed in opulence. Orbs of white and purple floated overhead, casting a soft glow throughout the hall. Purple, pink, and white roses flooded the room, the scent lovely and intoxicating. A trio of violins accompanied by a harp played the most melodious tune, and my forever mate stood ahead of me on a crystal-laden dais.

Alexander looked perfect. He wore a black suit with a long jacket, accompanied by a purple shirt of the same fabric as my dress. His long dark hair was shiny and smooth, worn loose down his back. He beamed with pride when he saw me, his eyes taking me in with love and admiration. His parents, Lord and Lady Kane, stood nearby. They were dressed in coordinating black and purple, their simple crowns made of brown antlers and rubies adorning their heads.

A chorus of bells sounded, filling the Great Hall. When they finished, a harp and a flute, joined by a violin, took over. I stepped into the room, making my way slowly and methodically to Alexander. He reached his hand out to me. I took it and joined him on the dais, facing him and holding hands. The tune faded out, and only the strum of a soft harp remained. Lady Sonia took her place before us, but I hardly noticed her. My eyes were fixed on Alexander alone, and his on me.

Lady Sonia began the binding ceremony, her voice droning in the background of my mind as I focused on my one true love—envisioning being with him intimately, ruling with him completely, and later raising a family.

Our first order of business as High Queen and High King would be an official tour. We would visit each province with a show of leadership and power, and opulence of course. After that, we would have a grand ball in honor of our union. Dignitaries from each province would be invited and treated to the most spectacular gathering. After a year of celebrating, we would settle into our reign and all of Faevenly would prosper under our rule.

"High Queen," Lady Sonia said.

Alexander squeezed my hands. "That is you, my love."

I blushed, realizing Lady Sonia was addressing me.

I angled my face toward her. She wore sparkling sheer gloves and lifted a long purple cord laced with gold and silver strands. She held it up to us.

"High Queen Malena Strong of Strong Haven of Faevenly, do you recognize the sanctity of this cord?"

"I do recognize the sanctity of the cord."

"Lord Alexander Kane of High Meadow, future High King of Strong Haven and of Faevenly, do you recognize the sanctity of this cord?

"I do recognize the sanctity of the cord."

"Today you present to each other the greatest of gifts—undying love." She draped the cord over our hands. "This binding will join two souls, two hearts, and two houses, forever." She wrapped one end up and over my wrists. "You will no longer be of one body, but of two, joined together forever." She wrapped one end up and over Alexander's wrists. "May the sun, the moon, and the stars bless you and keep you forever united."

As I gazed into Alexander's loving eyes, a force slammed on top of my hands. I whipped my gaze to Lady Sonia, then flicked my eyes down. A white powder doused the cord and my skin. Before I could utter a single word, my body soared into a free fall as everything and everyone around me faded away.

19 CELYSE

We raced from Lady Pen's home to the Sublands, stopping for only a few breaks. Rook took the lead with Leaf beside him. He knew the route, including a safe spot where he, Leaf, and Manny could wait while the rest of us went into the caves, an area called Road Rocks just outside the Sublands.

When the landscape morphed from lush and green to dry and rocky, I knew we were getting close. A few clicks later, I spotted the red, craggy, rocks lined up in a row.

"There it is," I said to Julio. "Like Rook described."

Coming upon the formation, we slowed to a trot until Rook came to a full stop. He hopped off his horse, and so did everyone else.

Manny moaned and groaned, walking in a circle, and stretching his legs. "Everything about horseback riding sucks."

Julio chuckled. "You're not entirely wrong."

"It is something you get used to, for sure," I agreed with a smile.

Manny rubbed his backside. "Well, I've had my fill. So when we get back home, and someone wants to do some horseback riding, I'm out." A weak trickle of laughter came out of him. "If we get back home."

"We will," Julio said quickly.

Rook and Leaf crouched on the ground and started moving small rocks and twigs around. Leto and Jaid stood close with their arms crossed and watched.

"A map," Leto muttered.

"Yes," Rook said. "I will show you a secret way into the caves."

We gathered around the Sublanders as they drew their replica village. When they finished, Rook took a stick and made an X at the westernmost edge. "We are here." He drew a small line in the sand going straight into the village but stopped before the drop into the canyon. He made another X. "Here is where you will find an outdoor market where vendors sell their wares. You can buy capes with hoods, and torches and flint. Celyse should stay hidden until the hoods are acquired. She will be recognized if seen."

He backtracked with the stick, then drew a loop around the outer edge of the city and made another X. "You will not go into the village but will stay on the outer rim. When you circle around, you will come upon a rock formation that looks like a chair." He drew a chair with square bottom, a square seat, and a round back. "If you face the chair and look to your right, you will see a large round rock. Move it and you expose a narrow entryway into the cavern tunnels. There is enough room for even the likes of me to fit into it. You all should be able to slip in easily."

"But to be sure," Leaf added, "You should take the bare minimum. A dagger each should suffice."

Leaning in with Julio, I studied the map. Getting in and out looked simple enough. The hard part would be enduring the whispering winds as we investigated why Draven was spending so much time down there.

"Wait a second," Manny said, pausing the chewing of his fingernails. "What if y'all go in, and Draven is there?"

"Never fear," Leto declared. "We will have our witch with us."

Looking at Julio, I could tell Leto's comment made him uncomfortable by the shift in his stance, but I agreed with Leto. Julio had great power inside of him, and he needed to trust his gifts. I grabbed his hand and squeezed. "A powerful witch."

"Okay, okay," Julio said. "I don't know about all that, but I'll do my best."

"There you have it," Leto said, clapping Julio on the back. "Your best is good enough for me."

Jaid and Leto started removing their bows, quills, and swords, and I removed my sword as well. The only thing they kept on them were their daggers. Julio had a dagger Rook had given him before storming Strong Haven West, and I still had the small black one Adva had given me. Looking at the dark hilt, I wondered what had happened to her and her brother.

"Everyone ready?" Jaid asked.

After a quick round of nods, Jaid, Leto, Julio, and I took off on foot. We walked with speed, wanting to get to the market before they packed up for the day. After a few minutes, red-canopied tents came into view.

Jaid stopped. "I will get our things. You all stay here."

Standing around a cluster of rocks, Jaid took off for the tents. It did not take long for him to return with four black cloaks. He tossed one to each of us, then held up two unlit torches.

"I will take one," he said. "Who would like the other?"

Leto reached out. "I will take the other."

I donned the cloak and lifted the hood over my head. Julio came up to me and tucked my silver strands back into the fabric. He smiled, his fingers lingering on my cheeks for a bit. "Looks good on you."

Resisting the urge to grab him and kiss him, I replied, "Thank you, Julio."

With our cloaks on, we stayed on the outer rim of the canyon like Rook had said, looping around to the west side. We made our way through the shopping crowd until we were the only ones on the pass. A crescent moon became visible but did not offer much light as the darkness quickly absorbed the sky and the temperature plummeted.

Jaid stopped, took out his flint, struck it, and lit the torches. He held it out. "Stay sharp for a rock that looks like a chair."

Studying the different formations, I saw arches, spires, and even a few holes. Finally, the chair came into view. It was big and bulky, made of sand colored rock with sharp edges and a round back. It reminded me of a chair for a god—a rock god.

We came upon it and studied it for a few seconds. "Wow, that's an actual chair," Julio uttered.

Leto pointed to a large rock on the right. "And that should be where the entryway is."

Jaid and Leto handed their torches to me and Julio, then heaved the rock out of the way, exposing a small opening.

Jaid took his torch back. "I will go first." He edged his way down, then crawled into the opening. With his light still visible he called out, "You can freely stand after you crawl in."

I was the next one in, followed by Julio and then Leto. Crammed together in the small space, I thought of the winds that tempted us to look down. We had told Julio about it, but I needed to give him another warning.

"Whatever you do," I urged. "When the winds come calling, do not look down. No matter what."

Julio did not seem to hear me. He kept glancing about in an odd manner, his eyes flicking around. "I can't help any of you. I'm sorry," he mumbled, raising his hands.

Thunderation. I grabbed his arm. "Julio, are you seeing spirits?"

"Yeah," he said with a swallow. "More than I've ever seen before." He struggled to keep his stare on me. "They're everywhere." He flinched. "They're swarming me." He closed his eyes. "Back off! Please! I can't help you!"

My heart broke to see him like that, struggling with spirits swarming him in such a small space. "You do not have to go in with us, Julio. You can go back with the others."

He pinched the bridge of his nose with one hand and drew in several long deep breaths. He moved his other hand to his shirt, where his cross hung underneath, a motion I had seen him do often.

He opened his eyes, forcing himself to keep his stare on me. "I'm okay. I want to help find out what Draven is up to. I'm your witch, remember?"

The bravery of his reply did not surprise me, but then his head jerked to the right. He stared straight ahead. "Draven?" he asked whoever he was seeing. He nodded. "My friends and I are trying to figure out why he spends so much time down here."

Leto, Jaid, and I stayed quiet while Julio listened to whatever the dead were saying. His eyes went wide. He turned to meet our curious stares. "They know where Draven goes."

"See?" Leto said with delight. "I never doubted our witch. Now Julio, ask if they will lead us to the spot."

Julio turned his stare to the space before him. "Can you?" He paused, his eyes widening a bit. "Oh, I see. Well," he gulped. "Can you show us?"

He waited a few seconds, then tore his gaze away from the spirits. "They're saying Draven goes deep into the caves and then disappears."

Leto raised his brow. "Disappears?"

"Yeah, they said they can show us where. They also said it's deep and dangerous. They also mentioned the winds."

Jaid extended the torch to Julio. "You lead, I will follow, then Celyse, and then Leto."

Julio took the torch. "Okay." He held the flame in front of him, then lifted his foot, holding it midair, as if the floor was moving and he was afraid to lower it. He waved his hand in front of him, as if clearing the way. "Please, back up. I can't walk with y'all on me like this."

He waited, then lowered his foot, and slowly started moving forward. "Thanks," he muttered.

"You got this, Julio," I encouraged. "Take your time."

With one hand on the torch and the other in front of him as if clearing a path, Julio took slow and methodical steps. The spirits must have started moving out of his way, because he gradually picked up the pace. He led us down a long tunnel that twisted and turned every which way, each step taking us farther down into the depths of the cavern. Every now and again he mumbled something. But I could tell it was directed at the spirits and not us.

"What are they saying, Julio?" Leto asked after a while.

"They're warning me to turn back. Saying we're crazy for going anywhere near where Draven has been."

"I am okay with being crazy," Leto said in a loud

tone, as if talking to the spirits. "It has served me well so far."

Julio chuckled.

"What are they saying now?" Leto asked.

"They're saying you will probably die first," Julio said.

Jaid had been mostly silent since Strong Haven West, but a grunt escaped his lips.

"You think that is funny, brother?" Leto asked.

"I do."

A whispering wind floated by, tossing my hair, sending a creeping shiver down my spine. My gut knotted. "Here come the winds," I warned. "Faster, Julio."

"Yes, faster, much faster," Leto called.

Julio broke into a easy jog, his light bobbing from side to side as the winds increased in speed, roaring around us like a sea of arrows. Unlike before, when they started out hard to hear, this time they screamed with clarity.

"Looooook doooooown!"

I bit the inside of my cheek, repeating Manny's mantra from our first time here, focusing on my running. "Eyes up, eyes up, eyes up."

We dashed deep into the cavern until Julio skidded, making a sharp right turn down a narrow opening. Jaid followed. When I turned, I collided into Jaid, and Leto into me. Julio had stopped in front of a dead end. We huddled close, as if standing together would somehow shield us from the menacing winds.

"The spirits are saying Draven disappears into this

wall!" Julio hollered, banging his fists against the rock. "Right here!"

The winds whipped wildly now, tossing my hair around my face. Spitting out a few strands, I placed my palms on the rock. I ran them every which way, my fingers scraping and probing. There had to be a nook or an opening of some sort. Everyone joined me, but we found nothing to grab. We resorted to pounding, as if our sheer strength could move the rock.

I grabbed Julio's torch. "Use your powers!"

Leto yelled, "Cover him!"

We moved in, as if our bodies could somehow protect Julio from the winds so he could call forth his magic.

"All right, then." He clenched his jaw and zeroed in on the wall. He blew out and placed his palms on the rock. He closed his eyes and his lips started moving. His face quickly fell into a relaxed expression, as if his thoughts had taken him to a place where there were no winds, no urgency, only a peaceful calmness.

"Come on, Julio," I whispered. "You can do this."

A soft blue haze trickled out of his hand. It hovered around his skin, like a glove, pulsing in a slow rhythm. It held a few seconds before shooting out a blue beam, spreading long and wide and covering the entire wall.

Jaid, Leto, and I gaped at the phenomenon, surprised and bewildered by the sight. He was doing it. With a few more pulses, the light and the wall vanished. Julio tumbled in and Jaid, Leto, and I lurched after him. Once we were through, the opening swirled shut.

Clambering to my feet, I gulped at the sight before me.

We were in a cave with blue iridescent walls. Even the ceiling was blue with rows of sparkling stalactites. Before us gleamed a small pool of dazzling water. The sound of the howling winds had vanished, replaced by the faint trickle of a stream.

Leto held the torch high. “Incredible.” He moved to the nearest cave wall. “Instead of rock containing aquoise, these interior rocks seem to be pure aquoise.”

Julio took my hand and pulled me to him, his eyes studying the cave. “Do you feel the vibrations?”

“Vibrations?” I held my breath, trying to detect whatever Julio was feeling, but could not. “I do not feel anything.”

“Nor do I,” Leto added.

“Nor I,” Jaid chimed in, inspecting the area with his torch.

Julio squeezed my hand, then let go. He walked to the water’s edge. He dipped his fingertips in and swirled them around. He smiled. “Wow, this is alive with pure energy.”

I crouched next to him and copied his motion. The blue water felt cool and refreshing against my skin, but nothing more. “How can you tell?”

He pulled his hand out of the water. “Once when I was little, my mom brought home this special jar of holy water one of her priest friends gave her. The priest told her it wasn't any ordinary holy water, but water infused with the essence of Jesus himself. He called it pure energy holiness. She poured some out so I could touch it, and it felt like this." He pointed at the water. "Tingly as if slightly electrified."

Jaid tilted his head. "I do not know these things you speak of."

I did not either, but Leto chimed in. "These are figures of an earthly religion. A priest is a teacher. Jesus is the son of a worshipped god."

I sucked in my breath and studied the water. "This water is made from the son of an earthly god? From the human realm?"

"No," Julio said with a shake of his head. "This water has nothing to do with my God or the human realm. But I think it has everything to do with Draven. As in, it's connected to his power source."

"Thunderation," Leto muttered, scratching his head. "It makes sense. Can you ask one of the spirits? See if they know anything?"

Julio surveyed the area. "None of them came in. I think they either can't come in or they don't want to come in." He paused. "Wait a minute, there is one lurking. He has just now showed himself."

"Ask him what Draven does in here," Leto said.

Julio faced the empty space. "Do you know?"

Julio listened. He nodded, then his eyes went wide, and he nodded some more. "Anything else?" he asked the spirit.

He waited a few seconds then said, "Wow, okay. I got it. Thanks."

Julio turned to us and relayed the message. "I was right. Draven strips his clothes, then goes into the pool of water and stays there for hours. Sometimes days. The spirit says he is regenerating. Like, charging his powers. When he comes out, he glows bright white, and before he steps out of here, the white glow gathers into his eyes. That's why his eyes are white."

"Incredible," Celyse whispered.

"More like terrifying," Leto said.

We all crouched down before the water, staring at the stillness, each of us lost for a second in our thoughts about Draven going in and what that did to him.

Julio said in a low tone, "We have to destroy it. Bring this whole thing down. And maybe, just maybe, we destroy Draven's power too."

Images of Strong Haven West crashing down jolted my brain, as well as a deep need for vengeance. "Yes," I agreed firmly. "We obliterate it."

Jaid kept his gaze on the water while he addressed Julio. "You think destroying this will destroy Draven?"

"I do," he answered. "If this is him, his life force or whatever you want to call it, then destroying this might destroy him. And with him out of the way, we take away Malena's most powerful ally."

Leto turned to Julio. "Do you think you can do it?"

Julio rubbed the back of his neck. "No way. Assuming I can even muster up that level of strength,

I'd probably die from the crashing rocks. We all would."

"There has to be a way," I mumbled. I paced around the cave, racking my brain for ideas.

"What about good old-fashioned explosives?" Leto suggested. "We can load up this place with enough chemicals to blow it to bits."

Julio perked up. "Y'all have stuff like that around here?"

"Most assuredly there are explosives in the Sublands somewhere. After all, their business is mining," Leto said. "Rook and Leaf will probably know where."

The idea of going back through the tunnels, gathering up explosives, and then coming back here made my stomach clench. As if sensing my internal struggle, Julio said, "I'll go. I'll take the torch and the spirits will lead me out. I'll go straight to Leaf and Rook and then bring back the explosives."

"I will join you," Leto said quickly. He turned to me and Jaid. "You two stay here and wait for us."

Jaid considered the plan for a few seconds, then nodded his agreement. And even though my mind riddled with doubts, I nodded too. I did not see any alternative. It would be faster and safer for two to go through and come back than for all four of us to go. Julio wrapped his arm around my waist and kissed me. I leaned into his soft lips and kissed him back.

"I'll be back," he said.

"As fast as you can, please."

He kissed me again. "Even faster."

Julio released me and joined Leto at the wall. With Leto holding the torch, Julio put his hands on the rock and used his blue power to make it vanish. With one last look at me, he and Leto stepped through, and the rock reappeared.

I stared at the spot, my heart calling out to Julio, *Please hurry back.*

20

LADY SONIA

My hands shook as I stood before Malena and Alexander. Their eyes had rolled back in their heads, but they remained standing. Flicking my attention to Lord and Lady Kane, I saw Maid Gidna fling powder into their faces, protecting her hands with the gloves I had given her, freezing them as they attempted to move from their place.

With the hard part of the job done, the music in the Great Hall stopped. No one uttered a peep as the enormity of what we had done fell down on us.

We had successfully pulled off an overthrow of the pompous egomaniac Malena, daughter of the High King and High Queen, and her puppet Alexander Kane.

Windon rushed forward. He stared at Malena and Alexander. "Is it over?"

I snapped my fingers in front of Malena's face. She did not flinch at all. I did the same to Alexander. He was just as still. "Yes, this part is over."

The room erupted in cheering as the maid servants and the guards celebrated. As much as I wanted to celebrate too, I could not. Our work was not done.

I issued an order to Windon. "Station a guard detail here in the Great Hall, over by the door."

He nodded. "Yes, Lady Sonia."

Gidna rushed over to me, excited and a little bit scared. "It worked, just as you said, Lady Sonia. The sleeping powder on the cord soaked with your herbal spell slipped them away. And the sleeping powder in the faces of Lord and Lady Kane ushered them to sleep."

I peeled off my gloves, making sure the powder did not touch my skin. Gidna did the same. "As long as you do not inhale the powder, or wrap that cord around your wrist, you are safe."

She backed away from the couple. "Oh, I am not getting anywhere near that cord."

Another maid servant with short-cropped brown hair with flowers woven into the strands came forward. Her name was Celia. "Lady Sonia, should I alert those hiding in the woods that they can come back now?"

"Not yet. I have seen that Lady Celyse is heading here. She travels with her human witch, Jaid, and others. We must hold our ground until she comes."

I did not mention that I had lost my sight of them, but that did not matter. I had to believe they were still on their way.

Gidna twisted her hands in front of her. "What if Draven comes first?"

The thought of facing Draven chilled me to the bone because I knew I could not even hope to compare to his strength. "We have to pray to the sun, moon, and stars that the human witch's spell will keep him away long enough for Celyse to arrive." Sensing Gidna's fear, I added, "We have to keep the faith. Especially now that we have made it this far with our plan."

She gave me a small smile. "Yes, keep the faith. I will work to do so."

I studied the cord I had used for my spell, marveling that I had successfully infused it with enough magic to cause whomever it was wrapped around to fall into a state almost as deep as being undead. But I thought I needed more cords in case they awoke.

"Gidna, I must prepare more cords. Will you assist me?"

She nodded. "Of course, Lady Sonia."

My gaze scanned everyone in the room as I said, "The guards will remain at the doors. Everyone else, retire to your quarters until you hear from me or Maid Gidna."

I stood by the door as everyone filtered out. Gidna and I were the last ones to exit. Before we left, I placed a hand on the young and eager Windon. "Thank you for your bravery and your loyalty." I met the eyes of each of the four guards standing with him. "All of you."

With a nod from Windon and the other guards, Gidna and I hurried to my quarters, where I had set up my herbs and remedies. I needed to get to work fast before anything happened.

This was far from over.

21
CELYSE

With our torch running low, Jaid and I decided to snuff it out. Luckily, the soft haze from the magical water cast enough light into the damp air that we did not need the torch. Which was good. I would not like being plunged into darkness in a cave deep inside a cavern. Especially one linked to Draven.

While Jaid paced about, I sat on a raised bed of solid blue rock. I ran my fingers over the smooth surface when my fingertips met a notch. I dug in with my nail, and a sizable chunk of aquoise came loose. Thumbing the piece, I brought it up and examined it in the dim light as best as I could. It was light blue, flat and smooth, and about the size of a coin.

“A piece came loose,” I said.

Jaid did not say anything as he continued his inspection of our surroundings.

I tucked the gem into my pocket, then continued running my fingers across the rock, seeing if I could get another piece, but there were no more grooves or notches. Rising to my feet, I drew out the dagger at my belt and started searching in earnest.

"If these have value, we should probably try to get as many as we can," I said.

I meandered around the perimeter of the water, searching the cave walls, but the rock was solid. I scraped the tip of my dagger up and down but found no other divots or uneven layers.

"This entire cave is solid," I uttered, marveling at the formation. "Pure, solid aquoise."

Glancing around for Jaid, I found him standing at the far end of the cave, arms crossed like he was on guard detail. He never could shake his duty. Even when we were young, he often assumed this pose.

I went back to where I had been sitting and eased myself onto the rock. My mind drifted to Julio and Leto, and even Rook and Leaf. I hoped they could find what was needed quickly, and I hoped our plan would work. But a doubting feeling niggled at me, telling me something was going to go wrong. I pushed it away before it could stick, reminding myself that we were the good ones. And good always triumphed over evil.

A chuckle came out of me as I thought of the irony of my thoughts.

"What is so funny?" Jaid asked.

"I was telling myself that we are good, and we will triumph over evil. But for all my life I was on the side of evil and did not know it."

"You could not know, Celyse. The High Queen was cunning."

"I guess," I said, studying Jaid. He wore his long silver hair loose at his shoulders, his hand resting on the hilt of his dagger, his violet eyes sharp and focused "How did you know, Jaid?"

"Leto told me. And when he did, I joined the effort to take down Strong Haven from within."

"But that included me,."

I detected a pause and a slight flinch. "It was my hope that you would somehow see the truth in all things. I am glad you did."

"And if I had not?"

"I would have found a way to tell you."

I pushed my silver hair away from my face. The cave was cool, but the humidity sent a stickiness across my skin. I slipped off my cloak, then tore the edge of the fabric and tied up my hair. I smiled at Jaid, thinking how lucky I was to have such a faithful friend.

"I am glad I did too. I am also glad to be here with you, Jaid."

He kept a stiff posture. "Are you?"

I blinked, unsure of why he would say such a thing. "Of course, I am glad to be with you. Why do you ask me that? You are my best friend."

He crossed his arms and turned away from me, inspecting the cave yet again. I lifted myself to my feet and went over to him. I wrapped my hand around his arm and pulled him around to face me.

"Jaid, why do you ask me that?"

He glanced down for a few seconds before he met my stare and said, "Would you not prefer the company of your human?"

My stomach dropped. My lips parted. I detected a

layer of hurt in his violet eyes I had not seen before. I slowly lowered my hand, my mind racing.

Did Jaid harbor feelings for me?

Suddenly, I saw my friendship with him from a different perspective—all the time we spent together, the laughs we shared, the dreams we told one another, the nightmares we whispered. When my head was in the clouds after meeting Julio, Malena had asked if I had set my sights on Jaid. I laughed at her, saying he was like a brother. And all this time I had thought I was like a sister to him.

Now I knew the truth.

"Jaid, I . . ." My voice trailed off because I had no idea what to say. Shock had taken my words.

His wounded eyes searched mine. "Why was I not enough, Celyse?"

My heart shattered and hot tears stung my eyes. I loved Jaid, I always had, but not in that way. He turned away from me.

"Jaid, please," I choked out. "You are so important to me. You always have been and you always will be. I cannot lose you."

"You will never lose me," he said. "But right now, I need to walk away from you."

He continued walking, examining the cave, while I went back to my rocky perch and sat down. I turned into the wall and wrapped my arms round my waist. Pain filled my heart, and my mind went numb.

All my life I had been surrounded by things I could not see—a mother who was not mine, a father who was not himself, a sister who thirsted for power, a kingdom established on fear and death, and now a best friend who loved me. I had often jested with Jaid that he did not see anything—but I was the one who had not seen things.

I felt as if I did not know anything anymore.

22
JULIO

Getting out of the caves was a whole lot easier than getting in because the winds didn't seem to care that we were leaving. They left us alone. With the help of the spirits, and with Leto on my heels, we dashed out as fast as we could, climbed out of the opening at the rock chair, and hurried back to Manny, Rook, and Leaf.

Manny smiled when he saw us, but his expression erased and a dark look covered his face when he noticed we were alone. "Where are Celyse and Jaid?"

"They're fine," I said quickly. "They're back in a cave, waiting for us."

"A cave?" Rook asked.

Leto explained. "We found a cave Draven visits; it is made of solid aquoise with an underground pool of water. We have learned it is connected to Draven's power source. Our plan is to blow it up."

"Uh, blow it up?" Manny asked, his eyes big as they looked from me to Leto and back to me again. "How?"

"With explosives." Leto gestured at Rook and Leaf. "That is where you two come in. We are hoping you can get some, and quick. Before Draven shows up."

Rook's nostrils flared and his lips curled. He raised his hand and clenched his fist. "Destroying Draven's power would please me greatly. I will gather the necessary items." He swung his stare on Leaf. "You alert the villagers. They must be vacated."

"That's right, blowing up that cave could level the entire village," I said. "I should probably help Leaf, then."

"Good idea," Leto said. "Julio and Leaf will go together. I will go with Rook."

"What about me?" Manny asked.

"You guard the horses," Rook ordered.

"Okay," he muttered, looking freaked out. "I can do that. But please hurry back."

"We will," I said.

Leaf, Leto, Rook, and I sprinted toward the village. I lost sight of Leto and Rook as they split off while Leaf and I ran down into the canyon.

Leaf started shouting. "Everyone out! There's going to be an explosion!"

"Out! Now!" I joined in.

Everyone was milling around, going about their business, but our words forced them to a halt. The townsfolk regarded us with curiosity and alarm, but they stayed where they were.

"Evacuate!" Leaf yelled at them. "Now!"

"Get out! There's going to be an explosion!"

Murmuring broke out. Everyone started scurrying. Leaf and I continued running and shouting, going deeper into the canyon, when suddenly I realized the structures of the village were all carved into the canyon.

"Out! Evacuate!" Leaf shouted.

I cupped my hands around my mouth and yelled, "There's going to be an explosion!"

Our shouts began echoing all around us as others chimed in, our warnings cascading throughout the cool, red-rocked canyon. We approached a configuration with massive stairs, a huge dais, and tall spires. It reminded me of a cathedral.

"Is that a church?" I asked, slowing down a tad.

Leaf followed my line of site. "The Caileans lived and ruled from there. I believe it is empty now. Down below are the cages."

"Cages?" Dawning recognition set in. "You mean, where you, Celyse, and the others were held?"

"Yes."

I stopped, my mind thinking of my dad and how he had been taken and enslaved and then died in Faevenly. I couldn't let that happen to anyone else. "We need to free whoever is still down there!"

"There is no one down there," Leaf said.

"Are you absolutely sure?"

He paused, then said, "I did not see anyone the last time I was there."

"Well, let's go check," I prodded. "Just in case."

Leaf cast his eyes down and shook his head a little. I could tell he didn't want to do it. I grabbed his shirt collar and pulled. "They're innocent, Leaf! And you're half human. Don't you care what happens to them?"

He batted my hands away and shoved me. "Fine, come on." And then he tacked on, "And do not lay hands on me again."

"Don't make me," I muttered.

We bolted to the stairs. A guard detail came out of an opening and charged our way. Leaf pulled out his dagger. With a gulp, I did too. Without giving us a second glance, they zoomed past us, but a guard with long silver hair skidded to a stop.

"Leaf! I thought you were dead!"

"Silas!" They hugged, clapping each other on the back. "I am well. But everyone needs to evacuate. We are going to blow an underground cave in the tunnels."

"You are the one who started the call for evacuation?" he asked.

"Yes, me and this human. But we need to clear out the prisoners if there are any. Can you help us?"

"You do not need help. There are no prisoners."

Leaf raised a brow and shot me a glance before following up. "What happened?"

"After Draven's and Alexander's display with the Caileans and then later the High King, and after you all escaped, the village revolted. Those loyal to the Caileans and Rook overthrew the Strong guards, and all remaining prisoners were set free. It only happened a day ago. I do not even think Malena knows."

My spirits lifted. "That's great news!"

"It will stop being great if we get stuck here," Leaf warned.

"If you are creating an explosion, then you are

right. It will most definitely not be great. Come on, follow me," the guard urged.

We started running the way we had come, warning everyone we passed to get out. Bodies were pouring out of the canyon, clutching their families and juggling armfuls of bags and belongings.

Panting, I said to Leaf, "Go back to Manny and the horses. I'll find Rook and Leto and help them set the explosives."

With a nod, Leaf continued with his friend and the crowd while I looped around to the rock chair. Sure enough, Rook and Leto were there. By the light of Rook's torch, I spotted two wooden boxes filled with twine and glass jars that looked stuffed with aluminum foil, and maybe some cotton.

Catching my breath, I pointed. "Explosives?"

"Yes," Leto said. "Explosives." He passed me Rook's torch, then said to Rook, "Go back to Manny and Leaf. We will join you when we finish."

Rook placed his thick hand on my shoulder, and the other on Leto's. "Good luck."

"Thanks," I said with a swallow.

Leto flung off his cloak. He placed one box on top of the other. He lifted them with care. "Slow steps, Julio."

I gulped, studying the jars. "Yeah, slow," I said, stripping off my cloak with one hand while holding the torch with the other.

We eased down into the tunnel opening, making small and precise movements. The spirits from earlier reappeared in a flash, but this time they didn't swarm me. Instead, they started leading me back to Draven's spot, waving me forward.

An old, shriveled man with dark skin came up close, wide-eyed, and pointed at Leto's boxes. "*¡Ay, Dios mío!* Those fae explosives will take this whole place down. I have seen them being used."

"I know. That's the plan," I said.

A younger stocky guy with blond hair piped in. "Plan? What plan?"

"To kill Draven," I said.

The spirits froze for a second, then started hooting and hollering, clapping with approval. But their celebration was short-lived when a breeze blew in.

"Get ready, kid!" a guy shouted from somewhere behind me. "The winds are coming!"

As if angry that we had returned, the winds whipped harder than before, sending granules of dirt and sand scraping against my face and neck. I shut my eyes, stopping in my tracks, then opened them to a slit. By some miracle, my torch still burned.

"Looook doooown."

"Don't listen!" one of the spirits hollered.

"Keep your eyes up!" another called out.

"Julio!" Leto called from behind me. "Are you okay?"

"Yes!" I hollered.

Forcing my stare straight and up, I bit my bottom lip, taking slow and easy steps as the gusts slammed into me from all sides. I thought I heard the clinking of glass behind me, and the idea of Leto dropping his boxes twisted my gut. I slowed my pace even more.

"Almost there!" a spirit yelled.

I plodded on until I finally came upon the sharp turn and the dead end. Edging my way forward, I stopped at the wall. The spirits fell behind, leaving me and Leto standing before the rock.

The winds shrieked. "LOOOOK DOOOOOWN!"

Shutting my eyes, I tossed the torch to the side and leaned forward, slamming my hands on the rough cave wall. I forced my mind to still as I directed my thoughts to my power. I envisioned blue light coming out of me, as brilliant as the sun itself. I thought of everyone who depended on me—Celyse, Manny, Leto, Jaid, Rook, and Leaf, along with everyone in Faevenly. I even thought of my mom and my family back home, and how I needed to get back to them. After a few more seconds, a pleasing warmth spread all around me. With a whoosh, I stumbled into the cave.

I spun around to see Leto rush in behind me, holding the boxes up and out with care as the wall swirled to a close behind him.

"Julio! Leto!" Celyse rushed over to me. She grabbed my fingers and squeezed, then extended her arms out to help Leto.

"Easy," he warned her. "These are highly explosive."

She removed the top box, while Jaid eased in and removed the other box. They set them on the ground away from us.

Leto brushed his long silver hair out of his face. "Well, that was fun." He flexed his hands and stretched out his fingers as we all gathered around the boxes. "But I hope to never have to do that again."

"What now?" Celyse asked, considering the glass jars.

Leto lifted the twine. "Rook said to tie this around the boxes, thread it out, and light it."

"We can loop it around in the cave, and then make a run for the exit after it's lit," Jaid said.

With everyone in agreement, we laced the boxes together as close to the pool of water as possible, then threaded the rest of the twine throughout the cave. When we finished, we stood by the wall, admiring our handiwork.

Jaid pulled the flint out of his pocket and lit the torch. He picked up the end of the twine. "As soon as Julio dissolves the wall, I will light it."

I nodded, then placed my hands on the wall. Before I closed my eyes, a wind dipped into the cave, a blur flashed by. I spun around with a start and saw Draven in front of us. His pale face almost glowed in the space, and his diamond-like eyes sparkled.

With his cape billowing behind him, he smiled. "How nice of you all to visit me at my home."

Jaid lunged with his torch to light the twine, but Draven zipped to him, wrenched the torch from his hand, zipped to the other side of the water, and tossed it in. He bent down and lifted a piece of the twine, and the whole thing turned to dust.

"And just like that, your plans are ruined." He dusted off his hands. "But you all must have known that, deep inside. In fact, I am willing to bet that none of you envisioned a scenario where this was going to work. And do you want to know why?" He paused for a few seconds, for dramatic effect. "Because nothing compares to me and my power. Not any creature in Faevenly, and most certainly not a lesser being from another realm. I reign supreme. I always have, and I always will."

"Get him, Julio," Leto whispered.

I held up my hands, focusing on my blue light, when Draven blurred into a frenzy of motion. His form bounced around the cave so fast I couldn't keep up. Suddenly, an arm wrapped around my throat. A fluttering of fabric blinded me, and I slipped into a free fall. Hurtling and soaring, my stomach lurched and my head spun.

And then everything stopped.

I blinked, trying to catch my bearings, when I realized I wasn't in the cave anymore, but in a dark wooded area. Cool, crisp air filled my lungs, erasing the moist humidity. The tallest trees towered above while Draven stood before me. He slammed his hands against my chest and pushed so hard my feet lifted off the ground. My body soared across the woods until I crashed against a tree trunk.

"Keep him here," he growled. Tree limbs crisscrossed over me, tethering me from head to toe to the bark of a trunk, and a wad of leaves stuffed into my mouth.

Draven flashed me a sinister smile. He leaned in toward my face and placed his lips at my ear. A blast of frosty cold came from him. "These woods are mine. It is triple warded on all sides. If anyone steps in other than me, they will die a painful death. And if you move, this tree will tear you apart. So be a good boy, will you?"

And he vanished.

Flicking my eyes about, I resisted the urge to tug and pull as I stood there in shock. My friends were in a cave with no way out.

And they were short one witch.

23
CELYSE

"No!" I yelled, rushing to the spot where Julio had been. I spun around, devastated that he had been taken by the likes of Draven. "Where did they go?!"

Jaid sprang to action. He dashed to the cloak he had set on the ground and started tearing. Leto caught on right away, snatching the one I had draped on the rock and doing the same.

"What are you two doing?" I asked.

"Draven may have destroyed our twine and plunged our torch in the water and taken our witch, but he left the explosives and I still have my flint," Jaid said.

"So now we have a new plan," Leto finished. "Blow the cave wall, then blow the cave."

Jaid nodded to his brother. "Fast, before Draven returns."

With my heart in my throat, I joined them in their efforts, tearing and ripping the fabric apart. When we had shredded both garments, we started tying them together, creating a long piece. Jaid gave each section a tug, then placed the boxes of explosives at the edge of the water. He took one of the jars and went to the spot where we had entered the cave.

"You two get back," he warned.

Leto and I scooted away and crouched down while Jaid unscrewed the top of the jar, placed a long piece of fabric in, and set the jar on the ground. He took his dagger and cut off a chunk of his hair. He set it on the other end of the fabric, then got to work scraping his blade across the flint, sending sparks onto his silver strands.

Striking again, and again, and again, his hair would catch a small flame, but quickly went out. Over and over he tried, adding more hair, striking the blade harder and faster, but nothing worked.

I rose from my spot, wondering if the damp air prevented the flame. Or maybe Draven had spelled the cave so that our efforts to get out would fail. Either way, it looked like we were stuck here forever, or at least until Draven returned and killed us.

"This is bad," I muttered to Leto.

He stood beside me, his expression grim. "You are not wrong."

Jaid echoed our sentiments. He pounded on the cave wall, then hollered as a sea of emotions burst out of him. I blinked, unsure how to react to him showing such deep feeling, when he picked up the jar, backed away, and hurled it at the stone wall.

Leto pulled me down and covered me as a blast rocked the cave and blinding light filled the air. We stayed low together, then slowly raised our heads. I waited for the other explosives to go off, but miraculously, they did not. Dust and debris floated in the air, clogging my throat and blocking my sight. I waved my hand in front of my face, desperately searching for Jaid, when he came into view. Black smudges smeared across his face, and his silver hair was covered in ash.

I leapt into his arms and hugged him. "You are all right."

"I am," he said, holding me with fierce intensity before he let go and stepped away. He motioned to the blasted opening. "Now, go. You and Leto. I will detonate the rest of the explosives myself and follow you."

"What?'" I asked, stunned. "No. It is too dangerous."

"I agree with Celyse," Leto added, grabbing Jaid's shoulder. "We must abandon this cave and get out of here while we can. There will be another opportunity for us to get Draven."

Jaid put his hand on top of Leto's, ignoring everything he had said. "Get a head start. I will be right behind you."

Leto shook his head. "Stubborn," he muttered under his breath. "If that is our play, then I will stay with you."

"You will not," Jaid shot back. "I need you and Celyse to get out of here. She will need you." He narrowed his stare. "Will you do that for me, Brother?"

Leto kept silent for the longest few seconds before he nodded. "I will."

Suddenly it felt as if time stood still. My heart tightened, my body trembled, and my blood chilled. Dust wafted around us as I studied the face of my childhood friend. "Jaid," I whispered, my eyes watering over because I did not think he could survive his plan. "Do not do this. I beg of you."

"Please, Celyse. Go," he urged. "It is the only way."

I kept my stare on Jaid as Leto pulled my arm, dragging me with him. In those last moments, Jaid's eerily calm and accepting gaze told me everything.

He knew he could not survive either.

Leto hurried me over the debris at the wall opening, then pulled me into the dark tunnel. Keeping one hand on his back, I followed him as the path twisted and turned. With each stride, I prayed to the sun, moon and stars for Jaid to be safe. I could not lose him. He was the closest thing I had to family.

An explosion rocked the tunnel, catapulting Leto and me forward like cannon balls. My body slammed against the dirt floor, my hands scraping against the jagged rock. I struggled to get up as stars littered my sight.

"Leto," I sputtered out. "Are you okay?" I reached out into the darkness, searching for him, when my fingertips met his.

He latched on and yanked me forward. "Yes! Keep going!"

We stumbled forward, struggling to catch our footing. With a sharp turn, a sliver of light came into view. We pumped our arms, sprinting toward the opening.

We wiggled our way out as the tunnel behind us collapsed in on itself in a booming whoosh.

Leto and I tumbled onto the dirt. I covered my head, protecting myself from any aftershock, struggling to catch my breath. When the calamity ceased, I lowered my arms and peered about, seeing nothing but dirt and rock. The mere sight of the destruction and what it meant pierced through me.

Jaid was no more.

Leto muttered something to himself, then got up and walked away. I buried my face in my hands, my heart breaking and my body heaving, as an ocean of tears gushed out of me.

I had lost Julio. And now I had lost my best friend.

24
DRAVEN

I sneered at the human witch, strapped to a tree and wrapped like a cocoon in my forest home. Revulsion for the foul creature boiled inside me, filling me with anger and disgust. I longed to end him but resisted the urge.

I might need him later.

Leaving him in his place, I moved away to the edge of my forest when a dryad of dark leaves and gray moss emerged from another tree. Bark fell from her branchy fingers with each timid step forward.

"Master Draven," she said in a low voice. "Would it not behoove you to end the human so you can remove your banishment and regain access to the palace?"

I spun around, my cloak flapping behind me. I stared down the dryad, outraged at the boldness of the creature to think it could address me, let alone give me counsel. When I spelled the dryads into revealing themselves so I could gain control of them, I threatened to destroy the trees if they did not do my bidding. I had never given them permission to speak.

Narrowing my eyes, I warned, "Know your place."

The dryad stepped away, blending back into the trees. "Yes, Master."

Whipping back around, I peered at Strong Haven Palace in the distance. Darkness shrouded the structure, yet a hint of light from the crescent moon provided enough illumination to see the ivory spires and glints of gold. The human witch had banished me from the palace, but his magic had waned significantly over the intervening days. And while the dryad was right that ending the witch would end the spell, I never gave up an advantage if I did not have to. I was near being able to enter Strong Haven on my own anyway. Now was as good a time as any to test my access.

I took slow, methodical steps forward when a tremble shook the ground. A violent gust whipped through the trees, sending birds scattering and leaves plummeting. The ground beneath my feet split, and pain like a scorching dagger shot through my body. Clutching my chest, I stumbled to my knees, knowing exactly what was happening.

My energy source, my precious aquoise pool, had been destroyed.

"No!" I roared. Fury raged through me. I should have never left Celyse and her fae allies alive in that cave. I should have gone back to end them once and for all. Clenching my fists, I pounded at the dirt, vowing to finish them off. But first, I needed to handle my new predicament.

My thoughts turned to Malena as I struggled to my

feet. I needed to claim the bargain she had struck before it was too late and my power left me.

With my cloak drifting behind me, I marched through my black forest. When I approached the line that separated Strong Haven from the wild, I paused. Surveying the manicured and pristine grass and shrubs beyond, I drew in a breath and stepped onto the lush grass. . . and waited.

"Well, well, well," I said out loud with a satisfactory exhale. "The human witch's spell has faded, and now I am back where I belong in time to claim what is mine."

I had missed Malena's binding ceremony by a day but smiled at the idea of giving her the glorious gift of aiding me.

Quickening my pace, I breezed through the gardens, making haste as I entered through the rear of the palace. Once inside, I stilled my senses so I could detect Malena's location—the Great Hall.

Rounding the corner, I marched down the corridor. When I entered the hall, a group of guards attacked. With a cry, they let loose a barrage of arrows. I lifted my hand with a swoop and cast out a blast of power, halting the arrows midair. I spun them around, then flung them back with a jerk, each one hitting its shooter square between the eyes.

"So brave, and so foolish," I muttered.

With the guards out of the way, I studied the surprising scene before me. The binding had been halted, frozen in time. Alexander stood on the dais, Malena across from him. Lord and Lady Kane were at their seats, mouths open in surprise. Nobody else was in the room.

I strode up to Alexander and Malena and circled them, examining them from all angles. “Did your precious house turn on you, Malena? Is that what happened here?” I glanced at their wrists and laughed. “Still wearing your binding cord. How lovely.”

Moving closer, I spotted clumps of white powder. “Ah, I see what transpired here.”

A pattering of slippers sounded on the marble floor as Lady Sonia rushed into the hall. She stopped when she saw me, then raised her hand as if to hurl a spell at me. I did not have time for amateur magic; I needed Malena.

In a blur, I zipped over to the palace healer. With a light touch, I placed my finger on her forehead and whispered, “Out.” She crumpled to the ground in a heap.

I returned to Malena, rubbing my hands together. “Now, where were we?”

I drew out my dagger, scraped off the powder from the cord, then cut the binding. Cradling her in my arms, I left the hall, traversed through the corridors, and climbed the main staircase. Bypassing her old room, I sensed she had taken up residence in the royal bedchamber and made my way there in earnest. As I entered the room, the smell of honeysuckle and roses engulfed me. The blue and silver color palette of the former High Queen had been replaced with pink and lavender. I set Malena on the bed and waited for her to awaken.

Her eyes fluttered open. She looked about in a daze before focusing on me. "Draven?" She sat up with a jerk, looking lost and afraid as she scanned the room. "Wh-wh-what is happening? I was being bound to Alexander and—" Her words got lost as she struggled to think of what had happened to her.

"You were spelled. By Lady Sonia," I said.

She gasped. "Lady Sonia?"

"Yes. It appears your staff is not as loyal as you thought. Luckily for you, my most prized possession, I came to your aid."

Ever the High Queen, she held her head high and pronounced, "I am grateful for your intervention. But I am no one's possession."

I took off my cloak, my long dark hair spilling out, and I studied her with intensity. "Oh, dear, sweet Malena," I cooed, trailing my finger down her soft cheek. "I own you, and you know it." I wrapped my hands around her wrists and held her down. "You asked for it."

She jerked from side to side, as if the motion would prompt me to move so she could get up, but I did not budge. "Where do you think you are going?"

She thrashed about. "I order you to let me go!"

I laughed, then brought my stare down on her. "I do not take orders from you. You command nothing and no one."

She silenced, as if she did not know what to do or

what to say. So I thought I would help her out. I leaned in and brought my face so close our lips almost touched.

"Malena," I said, enjoying the way her name rolled off my tongue. "You asked about my bargain with your mother, a bargain you assumed when you pleaded for my assistance."

She gulped. "I did not plead," she asserted with a boldness I almost admired. Then she added in a low voice, "But I did ask about the bargain."

Her curiosity knew no bounds. "Well, now it is time for you to know."

The young and ambitious High Queen Malena kept quiet, the sheer terror inside of her muffling her voice. The way I liked.

"In exchange for your father, and everything that came with being his betrothed, your mother bargained her life source." Malena gasped. She pressed her head back into the pillow, desperate to increase her distance from me. "I had not yet claimed it because I did not need it. But now, I do."

Her heart pounded against her chest so loudly, I could hear it through her ceremonial garb. Could see it pulsing through the vein at her neck.

"I will give you my firstborn," she blurted.

"I do not need your firstborn."

"I-I-I will give you . . . Strong Haven."

I smiled. "I already have Strong Haven."

Wrapping my hands around her wrists even tighter,

I admired her perfect pink lips. "Be still and this will not hurt . . . much."

I pressed my mouth on hers, grinding down on her as she kicked and writhed under me, screaming into my mouth. I held her steady, breathing in her sweet innocent scent, reveling in her pure taste, each spittle from her yells making everything about her more desirable.

I sucked in, taking a small swallow of her breath, letting it travel through me and into my lungs. So crisp, so young, so raw. Tightening my grip, I sucked again. This time my inhale was longer and deeper, satisfying my innermost primal need. And as much as I wanted to enjoy her and parse out each luscious mouthful of her essence, my desire could not hold back any longer.

Pushing my lips harder, I opened wide. Inhaling everything I could, I filled my mouth, swallowing her breath in wild gulps, extracting and taking until her body stilled and her mouth went slack. I held her to me, enjoying the aftershock of the last few puffs of her before I pulled back and gazed upon her wrinkled and hollow face.

"Thank you, Malena," I said, kissing her forehead. "Thank you for bargaining with me."

I took the blanket from the foot of her bed and covered her from head to toe. I lowered the orb lights that floated along the ceiling, snuffing them out and plunging the room into darkness.

Now it was time to visit the elder High Queen. I rubbed my hands together, delighted at the idea of claiming her life source too, not even needing her bargain as there was nothing she could do to stop me. It was a shame she would not know. But in the end, it did not matter, as long as I got what was mine.

Stepping out into the corridor, I focused on Anise Strong. Closing my eyes, I sensed she had been put in Celyse's old bedchamber. How fitting. I made my way to her quickly, excitement building with each step. And when I got to the bedchamber and entered, I found her laying atop the bed, dressed in all white, looking angelic and peaceful.

I walked to her and kissed her forehead. "My dear Anise, after all these years of us being together, it has come time for me to take your life source. But not from our bargain, as that has transferred to Malena and I have claimed her only moments ago. She was scrumptious and I took great delight in consuming her." I kissed one eyelid. "Now, it is your turn, and I am taking you because I have wanted you for so very long." I kissed her other eyelid. "Indeed, I have wanted you more than anyone or anything. For without you, I would have never known the depths of my greatness." I kissed her lips. "I will forever be grateful for you."

Prying her mouth open with mine, I slid my tongue in and laced it with hers, kissing her softly. She did not taste light and sweet like Malena, but was heady with spice and musk. Her flavor sent me soaring.

"Intoxicating," I whispered. "Like I knew you would be."

Craving more, I pressed my mouth on hers with

fervor, shoving my tongue in deeper, our connection driving me wild. With a guttural moan, I explored every inch of her mouth, swiping and probing and tasting and swallowing, taking my desire to the brink before I whipped out my tongue and sucked her air with feral force.

Growling with desire, I gulped and guzzled, taking her breath, enjoying every last pull of her essence as I filled myself with her life source. My body shuddered and my insides expanded as I emptied her completely. When her last exhale filtered into me, I sat back and closed my eyes, waiting for the tremble within me to subside, every inch of my body tingling.

"You are incredible," I said in a low voice, opening my eyes and admiring her shriveled face. "I will never forget you."

I crawled off her and sat in an oversized plush white chair in the corner of the room, not bothering to cover her so I could admire my handiwork. Although I felt rejuvenated and stronger than ever, I decided to rest, knowing Celyse and the others were sure to come looking for Julio.

And I wanted to be ready.

25
CELYSE

I could not speak, could not think, could hardly even breathe as Leto and I returned to Manny, Rook, and Leaf without Julio and Jaid. Worse was explaining to them what had happened. Especially Manny. He got so angry, he abandoned his easy manner and punched one of the rock formations, breaking his hand. Leto wrapped it as best he could, but there was no repairing the heartache.

We sat with our sorrow for a few moments at our enormous losses, but all too soon, the four of us had to decide our next move. There was no time to waste.

We had no idea where Julio could be, or if he was even alive. But if we were right about the aquoise, then Draven had either lost his power or was losing his power. That left Malena and Alexander. We knew without a doubt where Malena was, and it was likely Alexander was with her.

So we took off for Strong Haven, trusting that going there and confronting Malena would provide answers about Julio and even Draven.

It was our only next move.

Overflowing with despair, I forced myself to believe

Julio was somehow all right and would use his gifts to come back to me. As for Jaid, I did not think I would ever get over the loss.

We rode hard through the night and continued into the day. And when the sun again slipped from view and the stars and the crescent moon filled the sky, it was Leto that brought some sense into us.

"We have to stop," he urged. "We need rest, as do our horses, even if only for a little while."

With the rocky and rough terrain behind us, we found a grassy area on the east side of the Mother of Rivers that looked suitable for a stop. Fresh water flowed nearby, and bushels of strawberries grew in abundance.

We built a small fire, then sat around in silence, everyone lost in their thoughts. The fire popped and sizzled as I gazed at the flames in a trance of despair. If someone had told me my courting season would end like this, I would have never believed it. Yet here I sat, with my life shattered beyond repair. I did not even know myself anymore.

Leaf broke the silence. "What is our plan when we get to the palace?"

"Look for Julio," Manny answered.

"And if destroying the aquoise pool took away Draven's power, then we hunt him down," Rook added. "He would be a wounded animal, ripe for the killing. After that, we kill Malena and Alexander."

Staring at the crackling flames, I thought Rook was right about Draven. We needed to finish him off. But I did not know if killing Malena and Alexander was the answer, though I had no alternative suggestions. But I did agree that we should look for Julio.

He was my main mission.

"If we are in agreement, then that is the plan," Leto said. He rose to his feet and meandered away from the fire, then lay down under a tree with his hands folded under his head, his back facing us. Leaf and Rook did the same.

Manny rose to his feet. Before going to his own resting spot, he placed his hand on my shoulder. "We'll find him, Celyse. And about Jaid, I'm really sorry."

I nodded. "Thank you, Manny."

I sat with my sorrow while the minutes ticked away, my mind replaying every horrible moment in that cave. Eventually, overcome with despair and exhaustion, I lay by the fire and closed my eyes.

"Celyse," a voice whispered. "Celyse."

My eyes snapped open. I sat up with a start to see Julio sitting next to me. I lunged for him, my arms passing through him as my heart soared with relief.

"You are alive!"

He reached out his hands as if trying to grab mine. "Yes, I'm okay." He gazed about. "And you're not in the cave."

"No, we are not." My mind went to Jaid, but I pushed that aside, thinking Julio did not need to know about that right now. "We set off the explosives, and now we are headed for Strong Haven."

"I should've known. A massive earthquake shook

all around me, and Draven lost it. He screamed like mad and then stormed off to Strong Haven, I think."

"Strong Haven?" I asked. "You are near there?"

"I'm in a dark wooded area, and I'm being held by some sort of magical vine against a tree. I'm pretty sure I see the Strong Haven spires in the distance."

"Can you break free from the vines?"

He shook his head. "No."

I rose to my feet, eager to get going. Finally, something was going our way. "Keep trying. I will wake the others and come for you."

"No! Do not come for me. Draven said the forest is triple warded, and if anyone comes in, they'll be killed. And if I move, I'll be torn apart."

I placed my hand on my mouth, considering his words. "The forest is spelled."

"It has to be." He took a few deep breaths before he said, "You need to get to the palace and take out Draven while he's weak. That is the priority right now. Okay?"

I knew Julio was right. We needed to eliminate our immediate threat. But still, he needed me.

"Celyse, I'm not kidding. You must stop Draven now while you can."

"All right," I said, giving in. "I will come for you after."

"And I will be here after," he said with a smile. He reached out to my face. "Please be careful, babe."

Before I could say anything, he faded from view.

Galvanized with renewed energy, I shot into action. "Everyone! Wake!"

I kicked dirt onto the fire as the others rustled about. A pale light on the eastern horizon revealed the makings of a new day filled with fresh new hope.

"What is it?" Leto asked.

"Julio came to me. He is being held by magical vines near the Strong Haven Palace. He said Draven seems compromised by the destruction of the aquoise pool and has stormed off to the palace. We need to go there, now."

Manny sprang to his feet. "Julio is okay?"

"He is."

"Then let's go! He needs us!" Manny called out.

"We are going, but not to Julio. The forest where he is being held is spelled. We must eliminate Draven first and foremost. Then we can search for Julio."

"He said that?" Manny asked. "It's spelled?"

"He did."

"Julio is right." Leto came up close. "We must eliminate the threat before we do anything else."

"I agree, as well," Rook added.

"Fine, then," Manny said, giving in. "I guess it makes sense."

Rook and Leaf had gathered their things and mounted their horses, excitement and eagerness brimming in their eyes. Leto helped Manny climb onto his, then mounted his own.

"We must hurry," I said, spurring my horse into a run.

We galloped at a fierce pace, only stopping for two quick breaks. When the sun peaked high in the sky, the massive ivory-and-gold palace came into view, and soon we were on the main road to the palace. I thought of the last time I was on this road; I was in a carriage with a torn and soiled wedding dress. Now I was coming for vengeance. We all were. And we were ready.

We dismounted our horses and Rook took the lead, heading for the door with long, powerful strides, but stopped after a few paces. He turned around to face us. "Something is amiss."

My heart stopped as I scanned the palace, quickly noticing what Rook meant. "Guards," I uttered. "Usually there are guards out here, and there are none."

"Correct," Rook said. His nostrils flared as he unsheathed his dagger. We all did the same, holding our weapons in a defensive posture.

"Stay sharp," Leto warned.

Rook continued in the lead position. With a creak, he opened the door, and we filed in nice and slow. We stood in the entryway, looking about. There were no guards and no maid servants; in fact, not a sound could be heard.

"Where is everyone?" Leto asked in a low voice.

"I have a really bad feeling about this," Manny whispered.

"I as well," I said.

The stairs were in front of me, and just beyond were the glass doors that showcased the garden. To the right were the study, the music room, and the art room. To the left were the Grand Receiving Room and the Great Hall.

I flicked my dagger to the left. "We try this way first."

Rook nodded. "Stay together."

With Rook still in the lead, we passed the empty receiving room. When we reached the Great Hall, my stomach dropped. Five guards were down with arrows in the head. Lady Sonia lay crumpled on the floor. The Lord and Lady of High Meadow, Alexander's parents, were in their seats mouths agape and bodies still as statues. They were dressed in threads fit for a royal ceremony. Up on the dais stood Alexander, also in fine threads, also motionless.

"Thunderation," I muttered.

"What happened here?" Leaf asked.

"Somebody pressed pause," Manny muttered.

Crouching down on the ground, I checked each guard's neck for a pulse, but did not find one. Then I checked Lady Sonia and found a strong one. "Lady Sonia is alive," I said.

"Let us check Alexander," Leto said.

We strode over to Alexander. A binding cord draped from his wrist. I gasped, my mind suddenly realizing what was happening in the room. "They were having a binding ceremony."

Leto raised a brow and came over to me. He indicated the empty spot next to Alexander. "Then where is Malena?"

My mind raced with places where Malena could be when a pleasing whisper tickled the back of my neck.

"What the hell happened here?" Julio asked.

I spun around and saw Julio's shimmery form. "I do not know. We have only just arrived."

Manny ran to me. "Are you talking to Julio?"

"Wow," Julio said, circling Manny and waving his hand in front of his face. "I was concentrating on you, so I guess that means you're the only one who can see me."

"It appears so," I said, agreeing with Julio. Then I said to Manny, "He is right in front of you."

"Julio," Manny said, his eyes darting around. "Thank God you're alive!" He made a punching motion with his fist, and Julio made it back. Then Manny said, "Now that you're here, you need to use your witchy skills to figure out why everyone is frozen."

I eyed Julio. "Can you do that? Use your gifts for something like this?"

Julio circled Alexander. "Actually, maybe I can. My mom has allowed spirits to occupy her body for special readings. So maybe I can do the same thing, but the opposite. Maybe I can go into one of these bodies and see if they can tell me what happened." He came back to me. "Who should I try?"

"That one," I said, pointing to Lady Sonia. "She is the palace healer. She was never too enamored with the High Queen or Malena, so I think she can be trusted."

"Okay, I'll give it a go," he said.

"That one, what?" Leto asked, looking about. "What are you saying?"

"Julio is going to see if he can enter Lady Sonia's body and communicate with her as a spirit," I answered, my gut clenching tight. I prayed he could do what he said. If we were to defeat Draven, we needed information.

"Maybe we should pick her up and move her to the dais, then," Leto suggested.

"Good idea," I said.

Leto scooped her up and placed her on the dais, as if she were sleeping. Then he stepped back. "Tell Julio he can do his thing now."

"Go ahead," I nodded to Julio.

We stood back and I watched as Julio walked over to the healer, crouched down on the floor, then sank into her body. My eyes went wide. "Julio's spirit form has gone into Lady Sonia."

"Whoa," Manny whispered. "He's in there?"

"Hopefully, his efforts will work, and she can tell us what has transpired," Leto said.

"Before Draven returns," Rook added.

Manny started chewing his nails while Leto paced about. After not too long, Julio emerged.

"Julio is out now," I said for the others. Then I asked Julio, "Did it work?"

"Oh yeah, it worked. And get this, the staff was planning their own rebellion, and Lady Sonia was in charge. She used a spell on the binding cord to freeze Alexander and Malena. Then she used sleeping powder to freeze his parents. A lot of it, like a triple dose. They left them in this room to keep them contained and Lady Sonia began making more of her magical cords. But before she could finish, Draven showed up. He took out the guards, and when Lady Sonia charged in, he knocked her out with a touch."

I thought of the sleeping powder I wore at my belt. If I had been here earlier, I probably could have utilized it in some way to help. But we were too late.

"Does she know where Draven took Malena?" I asked.

"She doesn't know for sure, but guesses to her mother's bedroom. Malena has taken over that room now."

Julio paused while I relayed the information to the others. When I finished, Leto asked, "How did she spell her binding cord?"

Julio answered, "She didn't give a whole lot of detail on that, but she did say that if we remove the cord and loop it around Draven's wrist, it should work on him too."

I faced the others and explained what Julio had said, the realization of what Lady Sonia wanted us to do dawning on me. She desired us to get close enough to wrap the cord around Draven's wrist. Looking at the others, I saw on their faces that they understood that too.

Manny gulped, then verbalized what all of us were thinking. "Uh, is she saying she wants us to wrap that cord around Draven's wrist? As in, get close enough to him to do that?" He glanced at Lady Sonia. "Are you crazy, lady?"

We walked back over to Alexander, examining the cord dangling from his hand. Rook examined it with care. "I will do it," he said. "But one of you must stay close to Alexander, as he will surely unfreeze once I remove the binding."

Leaf drew out his dagger with a flash and pressed the tip against Alexander's jugular. "Nothing would please me more," the young fae said.

With Leaf in place, Rook approached Alexander. He tore off a chunk of fabric from his tunic, wrapped it around his fingers, then placed them on the cord. He carefully untied it by unwrapping it slowly and methodically. He tugged it away, freeing it completely, all while watching Alexander closely.

"Maybe he will not unfreeze right away," Rook said. "Stay keen, Leaf."

Leaf nodded. "I will."

Rook held up the shiny purple cord. "Now we only need Draven."

Leto rubbed his chin. "He will probably be here soon. And in his weakened condition, I think we can charge him and get that cord on him fairly easily."

"Weakened condition?" Draven asked from the entrance to the room. "What weakened condition?"

Manny let out a squeak and moved behind Leto, while Julio hovered close to me. "Crap," he and Manny whispered at the same time.

Draven pulled his hood down, showcasing his

perfectly pale skin, bright eyes, and long dark hair. He stood tall and looked strong and deadly.

"He does not appear weakened," Leaf whispered.

"That is because I am not weakened, Lord Kane. Or I guess I should say Sublander. You are not really a true Kane, are you?"

Leaf narrowed his eyes at Draven but stayed quiet as he kept his dagger on Alexander.

"You can kill him if you wish," Draven said with a wave of his hand. "I have no use for him."

Draven stayed where he was, then turned his nose up and sniffed the air. "Ah . . . one of you has a piece of my precious aquoise on them." He shrugged. "But as you can see, I do not need it."

I swallowed the lump in my throat, thinking of the rock I had put in my pocket when I was in the cave, wondering if Draven could tell that I was the one with it. Not that it mattered. It seemed he was not as dependent on the aquoise pool as we had thought. I wondered how he had kept his strength.

He steepled his hands together in front of him, tapping his fingers together. "Now," he said, licking his lips. "Which one of you should I kill first?"

Rook charged. Draven widened his stance and held his position, his eyes dancing with delight as Rook descended on him with a battle cry. Seconds before impact, Draven spun in a blur, letting Rook fly by, then kicked him square on the back, sending the Sublander crashing to the marble floor with a thud. Draven spun again, brandishing a pair of wicked daggers. He dove in and slashed at Rook's chest. Rook hollered as blood poured out all over the place.

Horrified at the sight, I had to act. With only a dagger and some sleeping powder, I knew I could not close enough to scratch Draven. So I did the next best thing. I grabbed my dagger by the tip and threw it. Draven swished his cloak, batting away the weapon with ease.

"Is this all you have?" Draven shouted with glee, seeming to enjoy himself. "Come on now!"

Leaf roared. Pushing Alexander out of the way, he rushed Draven with his raised dagger, and Leto joined him. Draven smiled, then flapped his cloak, but Leaf was ready. He slid under the dark fabric, popping up on the other side, ready to plunge his dagger in Draven's back, but Draven flipped in the air. He landed behind Leaf and sliced the young fae's back. Leaf tumbled to the floor with a howl of anguish. But Leto got through. He ducked around to the other side of Leaf, lunged in with his dagger, and nicked Draven's cheek.

Draven scowled, wiping the blood from his cheek, circling Leto with his dagger drawn. "I am finished with games," Draven sneered. "You will be the first to die."

Gasping with horror at all the blood on the marble floor, and scared Leto was next, I spotted the binding cord.

"The cord!" Manny urged. "Get it!"

Draven's eyes flicked to me, then to the fabric on

the floor. He licked his lips, eyeing the fabric as he twirled the dagger in his hand. "Who is going to make a move for that cord, I wonder? Rook and Leaf are minutes away from bleeding out, so it will not be them. The scrawny human is too weak to do anything. Leto is considering a move—I can see it in his eyes—but he is trying to be calculating." He pointed his dagger at me. "And you, half-blooded fae Celyse, you are filled with too much anguish over the human held captive in my forest." He glanced about, then added, "And where is your faithful puppy Jaid? Where has he disappeared to?"

My face must have given away my emotion, because then Draven added, "Oh my, have you caused his untimely demise somehow? Poor, poor Jaid."

Years of fearing and hating Draven exploded inside of me. Letting my emotions take over, desperately wanting to kill the witch to avenge Jaid and free Julio, I dove for the cord. So did Draven. Our hands connected on the silk material at the same time, but his grip was tighter than mine. He yanked the cord from me, then slammed his other hand around my throat. He climbed to his feet, dragging me up with him.

He cast a menacing stare at the others. "Move and I kill her."

Staring into his face, I knew his warning did not matter. I was dead no matter what.

26
JULIO

While Rook and Leaf lay bleeding on the floor, Celyse dove for the cord, but Draven edged her out. Now he had her by the throat. She grunted and clawed at him, thrashing her legs in the air, struggling for breath.

I rushed Draven, focusing on blasting my blue power at him with a punch, but I soared right through him instead. Leto and Manny charged too, but Draven unleashed a blast of red from his palms, sending them crashing across the room.

Celyse flashed me a look, the kind that was filled with sorrow and regret. Almost like a goodbye.

"No, you don't, Celyse!" I yelled. "Don't you give up!"

My mind raced and my eyes flicked about as I scrambled for what to do. My gaze landed squarely on Lady Sonia and a crazy idea formed in my mind.

I dashed over to Draven and stood in front of him. I glanced at Celyse for a second before taking a deep breath and stepping into the witch. A cold blast whipped through me as I stretched my arms and legs into his, taking over his body.

"Get out!" Draven screamed inside my head. "Out!"

Ignoring him, I focused my energy on his hand, prying open each finger one by one. When it fully opened, Celyse dropped. She fell to the floor, coughing and heaving. She held her throat, peering up at Draven.

"Julio? Is that you?"

"You will die for this!" Draven hollered. His words ripped through me with such force I thought my head might explode. But I refused to leave his body until the others were safe.

"Cord," I managed to squeak out through Draven's lips, almost unable to hold on any longer while the mad witch blasted me from within. "Get . . . cord."

Recognition lit her eyes. She leapt to her feet. Stretching her sleeve around her fingers, she yanked the cord still dangling from Draven's hand. She wrapped it around his wrist and tied it with a yank.

I fell out of Draven's body, shuddering as I left his cold and dark mind, then stood next to Celyse. Manny and Leto gathered too. Leaf and Rook stayed on the ground, cradling their wounds. We gaped at Draven, waiting to see what would happen with the cord on him, holding our collective breath to see if Lady Sonia's magic would work.

Draven's eyes were closed. His breathing stilled. His body stiff.

"Is he . . . frozen?" Manny asked. "Did it work?"

Draven's eyes snapped open. His lips curled. He

made a guttural noise as he thrashed and lunged forward.

Celyse moved for the dagger at her waist, but it wasn't there. She had thrown it earlier. Another idea must've sprung to her mind as she opened her pouch, dug in, and doused Draven's face with a handful of sleeping powder. She scooped again and slammed a heap on the binding around his wrist.

Draven's eyes rolled back in his head. He teetered, then fell over like a tree and crashed to the floor with a thud.

No one spoke as we all stared at the witch in shock. Not even believing our eyes.

"Holy hell," Manny whispered. "Is it done? Is he really, like, knocked out?"

Leto nudged Draven's leg with his foot. "I think so."

Manny clapped Leto on the back, then hugged Celyse. "We did it!"

Celyse beamed, then said to me over Manny's shoulder, "Julio did it."

Leto pulled his sleeve and wiped Celyse's fingers, "In case you accidentally ingest any of the powder."

"Good thinking," she said.

I moved in closer to her, when a roar filled my ears and a tug pulled at my chest. My spirit whisked out of the hall, returning to my body with a start as the criss-crossing vines released me. I fell face first into the dirt. I spit out bits of leaves and dirt, thinking this was the third time I had face planted in the last week. Or was it my fourth time? I had lost count.

I clambered to my feet and dusted myself off. I surveyed the dark forest, feeling sorry for the dead and decaying trees, but then noticed something. Sunlight started trickling through the forest canopy. Slowly at first, it soon began pouring down like the brightest summer day. Shielding my eyes, I marveled at the warmth filling the space.

Hues of green began taking over the dark leaves, like a wave of rebirth. The flaky and moldy black trunks hardened to a rich reddish-brown color. I thought of Genova, the dryad I had met at Leto's. I thought these trees were like her, and I knew she'd be happy at the change in the forest.

"You're free now," I said to them. "Draven won't hurt you anymore." Not knowing what else to say, I added, "Thank you."

Spinning on my heels, I took off for the palace. Not long after, I skidded through the front door and worked my way to the hall where everyone was. Celyse spotted me and rushed my way, wrapping me in a tight hug.

I held on to her for a long while, then pulled back and brushed her hair out of her face, kissing her softly on the lips. Manny came over and wrapped his arms around the both of us. After a long group hug, I pulled away to see what was happening. Lady Sonia knelt on the floor, binding more cords around Draven's wrists. The sight of him motionless and powerless shocked me, and I couldn't help but stare.

"Weird, I know," Manny said.

I rubbed the back of my neck. "Beyond weird."

"And I got to knock out Alexander," Manny said with a smile.

I tilted my head. "You did what?"

"He woke up and everyone was standing around and I was the only one that saw him, so I smashed a chair over his head," he said.

The biggest laugh rushed out of me as I imagined Manny with his fro hurling a chair at Alexander. I clapped his back. "That is awesome." And then I added, "But wait a minute, why is your hand wrapped?"

"Oh," he said, lifting it up. "I broke it and Leto wrapped it for me after the whole cave thing."

"Um, dude. You clobbered someone with a chair with a broken hand? Niiice."

Nearby, a team of young fae crouched next to Rook and Leaf, applying creams to their wounds and dressing them with bandages.

"Where is the knocked out Alexander and his parents?" I asked Celyse.

"Taken to the dungeons until we can figure out what to do with them," she said. "Draven will join them, after he is properly doused with Lady Sonia's spelled cords. He will not be waking any time soon."

Leto came over and patted me on the back. "I never doubted the skills of our witch." He placed a hand on Celyse's shoulder. "Or the resourcefulness of our princess."

One of the guards came up to Leto. "I am so

relieved to see you. It was not easy maintaining a ruse with the likes of Malena." He looked around. "But where is Jaid? I have not seen him."

Leto stepped back and shook his head. "He did not make it."

I turned to Celyse. Draven had said something about Jaid, but I wasn't sure if what he'd said said was true. "Jaid didn't make it?"

"He did not," she said with watery eyes.

I wrapped her in my arms. "I'm so sorry. I know how important he was to you."

We stayed like that for a while before parting, but stayed close. I scanned everyone's faces, realizing someone else was missing.

"Where's Malena?" I asked.

Lady Sonia piped in. "She moved the elder High Queen into her bedchamber and assumed the royal bedchamber for herself and Alexander. I believe that is where Draven took her."

I took Celyse's hand and squeezed. Even after everything Malena had done, they were still sisters. And if my gut was right, Malena was dead. Otherwise, she would have been down here, desperately trying to keep her claim to the throne alive.

"How do you want to handle this?" I asked Celyse.

She lifted her head and drew in a deep breath. "I would like for you to accompany me upstairs."

Leto and Manny moved aside as Celyse and I made our way out of the Great Hall. She led me down the corridor, up the stairs, and to a room with a wooden door adorned with intricate carvings. She released my hand and slowly pushed the door open.

Darkness shrouded the room and a powerful scent of spring flowers assaulted me. After my eyes adjusted, I detected a trickle of light from the edgings of closed curtains. A bed came into view, and on top, a body covered in a sheet.

"There she is," Celyse whispered.

She let go of my hand and took slow, soft steps forward. I followed but kept my distance, giving her space. She reached the edge of the bed, then slowly pulled back the sheet. She drew in a sharp gasp at the sight.

Malena's very life had been taken away; only a shriveled shell remained.

"How?" I muttered. "How did that happen?"

Celyse lowered her hand. She put the sheet back where it was and turned away. "There is a rare breed of fae called soul vamps. I thought they were extinct, but it looks like Draven is one."

"Soul vamp, as in vampires?"

"Yes. It is a breed that takes souls. Draven must have had no further use for her if he did this. I imagine he did the same to the undead High Queen, wherever she is."

As if Faevenly wasn't strange enough, now it had fae vampires. I wondered what else it had that I didn't know about.

I let her stay in her thoughts for a while before I asked, "You okay?"

"I will be." She straightened her posture and took my hand, her beautiful face filled with a myriad of emotion—sadness, hurt, and maybe even a glint of guilt. "We should go back to the others," she said. "There is much to discuss."

Everyone had left the hall except for Manny, Leto, Rook, Leaf, and Lady Sonia. Celyse and I joined them and we sat together, speechless and stunned at everything that had happened.

A maid servant came in with a tray of tall crystal glasses filled with lavender liquid. I took mine and sipped. The refreshing drink pouring through me, instantly making my tired and achy bones feel tons better.

"What now?" I asked, thinking Manny and I needed to get back to our realm, and hoping Celyse would come with me.

"Well," Leto said. "While you were checking on Malena, I checked on the former High Queen. It seems her soul has been taken from her and she has passed on."

"Malena has passed as well, in the same manner," Celyse explained.

Leaf stitched his brows together. "By Draven? He is a soul vamp?"

"Yes," Celyse said. "He must be."

"Incredible," Rook muttered. "How did no one know this?"

"How can anyone know the ways of such a cunning being?" Celyse asked.

Manny opened his mouth to say something, but I waved him to silence. The conversation was serious and didn't concern me or Manny. At least not yet. I could tell him about fae vampires later.

"What of Draven?" Rook asked, his face pale as he cradled his chest with his arm. "What will become of him?"

"I believe that is up to Celyse," Leto answered. "His wrongdoings were against her house, and she is the last surviving member."

Celyse must have been thinking about what to do with Draven, because she answered right away. "He will remain in his state of sleep, locked in a dungeon, sealed off from the world until he expires."

"Yes, my lady," Lady Sonia said. "He is already there and will remain so. I will see to it myself."

My stomach dropped because it sounded like Celyse was stepping into the role of High Queen, which meant she'd be staying in Faevenly. I felt so dumb for thinking otherwise.

"And you, Celyse? Will you be the new High Queen?" Lady Sonia asked.

"I am a Strong, and I will always be a Strong." She paused. "But I am also half human and wish to explore that part of myself." She looked at me. "If I can find someone to take me, that is."

My spirits lifted as my heart swelled. "I can totally take you."

Leto smiled. "I think that is a splendid idea. I loved

my time in the human realm. But now that I am here, I will probably stay a while."

"Perfect," Celyse said, "as I desire to leave Strong Haven in your care, if you will accept. You can even bring a certain red-headed fae to the palace if you wish."

Leto crossed his arms, looking a bit smug. "Lord Letormis. I rather like the way that sounds. And even better that I can have a guest," he said with a wink. "I guess I accept, then."

With the mood lifted, Celyse turned her attention to Rook and Leaf. "What of you two?"

Rook answered. "Leaf and I will return to the Sublands and rebuild. The Caileans were good and honest, and we will continue what they have started—building a land based on opportunity and acceptance for all."

Leto looked inspired by Rook's desire to honor the Caileans and chimed in with his own plans. "And I will work to usher in a new peace amongst the Council of Five, expanding it to the Council of Six so as to include the Sublands. I will end the ridiculous death sentence attached to the shimmers, and I will make sure all fae, whole-blooded or half-blooded, are treated equally. And every province will prosper and be free!"

Rook raised his glass. "Hear hear!"

I raised mine too, as did everyone else. "Hear hear!"

With the celebrating over, and with Celyse taking care of a few things before we left Faevenly, I went out in the back garden with Manny. Magic radiated from every inch of Strong Haven—it was in the vibrant green of the grass, trees, and shrubs; the heavy perfumes of the flowers and herbs; the bright blue of the sky; and the sparkling white of the puffy clouds.

Celyse had already spent some time with me back home, but I suddenly feared she wouldn't like it there.

"I can't believe you are bringing home a princess," Manny said. "A princess! What did your mom say?"

"My mom is excited to meet her. She says our house will be her house. *Mi casa es su casa.*"

I had visited my mom in spirit form before coming out into the garden with Manny. She completely lost it when she saw me, crying hard because she thought something had happened to me. But when she found out I had found Manny, and that we had defeated the evil witch, she was thrilled. And when I told her how Celyse wanted to come and had no family, she was eager to take her in.

"Your mom is the coolest," Manny said.

"Yeah, she is," I agreed.

We were enjoying the breeze and the fresh air, talking about everything that had happened, when Leto caught up with us.

"Julio, there you are," Leto said. "I have been looking for you." He glanced at Manny. "Mind if I steal Julio for a little while?"

"Go ahead. I'm gonna wander my way over to the

kitchen. See if there's anything to eat. Come find me when y'all are done."

Leto and I strolled on ahead, not saying anything for a bit. "Well, Julio, a new adventure awaits you back in Austin, and I have a couple of things I would like you to have."

"Really? What?" I asked, surprised at the offer, wondering what Leto could possibly be giving me.

He stopped and faced me with a serious look on his face. "First, my land. Second, the bakery. And third, my car."

I blinked, completely shocked at everything he wanted to give me. "What? You want to give me your land, your car, and a business?"

"You will need these things more than I. You and Celyse can rebuild the cottage, and you can run the bakery while you go to college. Celyse can work there too."

"I-I-I," I stuttered as I searched for the right words. "I am so grateful. Thank you so much, Leto."

He smiled. "You are most welcome." He fished out a necklace from under his shirt that I hadn't noticed. He took it off and handed it to me. A small key was attached. "This key opens a lockbox buried under the seventh plank of the dock at the lake. Everything you need will be in there."

"Thank you again, Leto." I slipped the necklace on with my other one, and then chuckled.

"What is so funny?" he asked.

"I'm laughing because you hated me when I first

met you. You even tried to throw me out of your house. And you had all that hair, and you were so grumpy, and I thought you were an old dude."

Leto smiled. "Ah, yes. I remember our first meeting fondly, and my haggard appearance. But look at us now."

"Yep," I agreed, "look at us now."

He placed his hand on my shoulder, and I did the same to him. He took on a serious expression. "You are quite a powerful witch, Julio, and I am proud to call you friend. Please do not lose your gifts. You never know—you may need them one day."

"Of course," I nodded, realizing he was right. "Thank you, Leto."

Leto and I went back to the palace and caught up with Manny. He was sitting in the kitchen with the staff, munching on cookies, telling stories of everything that had happened to us. The petite fae oohed and ahhed over his tales, and Leto and I chimed in with our own embellishments.

But all the while, I was secretly praying to God, thanking Him for getting us through everything.

We almost didn't make it.

After a while, and after a round of goodbyes, Manny, Leto, and I left the kitchen and meandered through the palace. When we got to the front door, Celyse was coming down the stairs with a packed bag. She was showered and changed, looking beautiful in a long, flowy purple dress.

"I am ready," she said excitedly.

"Us too," I said.

Lady Sonia hurried over to us, dashing down the corridor. "I have your serum, Lady Celyse!"

"Ah yes, thank you," Celyse said. She took the large black bottle that looked like a medicine bottle. She unzipped her bag and nestled it in with her things.

"One drop a day," Lady Sonia instructed. "And if you should need more, you know where to find me."

"I do. Thank you again." Celyse hugged Lady Sonia, and then Lady Sonia went on her way in the direction of the kitchen.

I raised a brow. "A serum?"

"It will allow me to age at the rate of a human," she said.

"Oh," I said, remembering that she had told me how fae age way slower than humans. "That would be good for our relationship." I laughed.

"Yes, it would." She smiled back at me.

Leto held out a shimmer. "Here it is, the last thing you will need. A shimmer that will take you to my place on Lake Travis."

Leto pulled open the shimmer, stretching it out long and wide. "Collapse it on the other side and keep it for when you want to come back," Leto said. "I would love a visit every now and again."

"We will most definitely visit. Don't you worry," I said.

"And when they come, I'll be coming too," Manny added.

"I expect nothing less," Leto said. Then he nodded.

"I will leave you all to it, then." He walked back toward the garden, leaving me alone with Manny and Celyse.

I looked at Manny. "Well, I think you should go first."

"You don't have to tell me twice. See y'all on the other side," he said, quickly dashing through the glowy mass.

Celyse faced me. She bit her lip, looking nervous. "I am excited but also afraid."

I rubbed her arms. "Don't be. I will be with you every step of the way. No matter what."

She moved in, took my hands, and gave them a squeeze. "You promise?"

"I promise," I said, kissing her softly on the lips. "Forever."

She picked up her bag with a deep breath, and together we stepped into the shimmer, and into the human realm, to a bright new future together.

27

DRAVEN

Settling in for a long sleep in a dark dungeon deep under Strong Haven Palace, I had no other choice but to wait for Lady Sonia's spell to wear off. For it would surely wear off over time. I could sense the weakness in her lesser magic and the flaws in her fragile potion. Her pitiful efforts to keep me in stasis would fail, and the foolish woman had no idea.

As I slumbered, my mind churned with all the ways I would punish my wrongdoers.

First, I would incinerate Strong Haven Palace, turning its inhabitants to dust. Next, I would track down Leto, Rook, and Leaf. I would torture them in the slowest and most gruesome manner, then cut out their hearts.

I would save the best for last.

I would cross into the human realm and hunt down Julio and Celyse. They would beg me to kill them quickly, but I would not. They did not deserve any such mercy. My mind pictured all the ways I would inflict pain on them.

At the end of it all, I would cut out their hearts too.

If it took me years to escape my dungeon, and Julio

and Celyse were no longer alive, I would exact my revenge on their bloodline, cutting out the hearts of their every last descendant.

They thought this was over. They thought they had won. Nobody crossed me and did not pay.

Nobody.

CONCLUSION OF BOOK TWO

This isn't the end.
It's only the beginning of what comes next.

Continue the journey in *Fae Hunted*
The consequences are only just beginning.

Start Book 3 now.

FAE BLOODLINES SERIES

Fae Away, book 1

Fae Fractured, book 2

Fae Hunted, book 3

Fae Rising, book 4

For a full listing of Rose's books, visit her website.

www.RoseGarciaBooks.com/GARCIAVERSE

Subscribe to Rose's newsletter.

www.rosegarciabooks.com/newsletter

Fae Bloodlines Series

A ROYAL ROMANTIC FANTASY SERIES FEATURING HISPANIC CHARACTERS, POWERFUL FAMILIES, DYNAMIC FRIENDSHIPS, AND FORBIDDEN ROMANCE

ACKNOWLEDGMENTS

Fae is the word!

I am so very glad I started writing fae fantasy because I am LOVING IT! There's something so incredibly exciting about a world that overlays our own and is filled with beautiful people, breathtaking scenery, and magical creatures. If Faevenly were real, I'd want to go there! I hope you feel the same way!

Now, about Fae Fractured… My favorite part about this book was writing Malena and Draven. It was so much fun breathing pure and unadulterated wickedness into everything they said and did. *Mwahaha*. I'm really looking forward to expanding on this in Fae Hunted. Make sure to continue the series to see what I mean!

Now, on to the acknowledgements…

First and foremost, I have to give thanks to God for keeping me and my family safe and healthy. I don't mention religion much because I consider it to be a very personal thing, but faith is a big part of my life. Much like it is with the Avila family!

I also want to give a HUGE shoutout to my husband, and here's why. I'm not gonna lie when I say

Fae Fractured was a challenge to write. I wanted to take you, the reader, on a journey to new and incredible heights with this world, these characters, and this story. But it wasn't easy. I actually had a lot of writer's block. EEP! Luckily for me, my husband is my secret weapon! (I guess, not-so-secret weapon, lol.) He is extremely well read and is a great resource for me. Always has been. So, when I needed help, I closed my laptop, turned to him, and together we hashed out the story. I'm so very thankful for him!

My writer besties, the Queens of the Quill, once again provided much needed cheering and motivation when I needed it most. I honestly cannot imagine muddling through writer life without them. They're the best!

To my reader group, The Rose Bud Society! Rose Buds, thank y'all so much for all the love, support, and encouragement! I am blessed beyond measure to know each one of you. Thank y'all so much for hanging with me on our FB page and, most importantly, for reading and loving my books! You make this whole writer thing so worthwhile for me!

To my INCREDIBLE editor, Liz Ferry! Liz, honestly, you complete me! Lol You are the bestest editor ever, and I'm so grateful to have you on my team. And, like the dedication says, I'm so glad your early is my late! I appreciate you more than I can say!

I can go on and on with thanking people, but I'm sure you don't have all day or night to read these acknowledgments. So let me just say, for those who've cheered me on and supported me, thank you, thank you, thank you!

ABOUT THE AUTHOR

Rose Garcia is a USA Today bestselling author and screenwriter known for crafting heart-stopping fantasy stories where belief is power, love defies all, and hope burns brightest. Magic is real in her world—and the only thing more dangerous than a broken heart... is a hopeful one.

A lawyer turned writer, Rose weaves stories of complicated romance, powerful families, deep-rooted friendships, and ancestral magic drawn from her Mexican American heritage. Her diverse heroes are driven by bold hearts, forced to confront tangled destinies and make impossible choices.

When she's not writing, you can find her designing escape rooms for her husband, obsessing over fantasy shows, traveling, or hanging out with her needy and precious rescue dogs.

Rose lives in Houston, Texas, and believes tacos are a core food group—because well, they are.

Welcome to the Garciaverse!

For more on Rose, visit www.rosegarciabooks.com.

Join Rose's FB Group

www.facebook.com/groups/TheRoseBudSociety

Subscribe to Rose's newsletter

www.rosegarciabooks.com/newsletter

www.ingramcontent.com/pod-product-compliance
Lightning Source LLC
LaVergne TN
LVHW010603100826
845148LV00014B/2831

* 9 7 8 1 7 3 7 3 2 6 7 1 7 *